Dragonseeds

Dragonseeds—crouching like some menacing beast on the cliffs above the sea: that was how the fortress home of her Tregellas kinsmen seemed to Ruth at first sight. And there was danger within its granite walls, despite the veneer of beauty. Did it come from the arrogant Dominic, with his hard eyes and barely concealed scepticism, or Grandfather, manipulating all their lives from his wheelchair? Was Bella's placid face a mask for resentment and hatred on behalf of her son, Simon, whose inheritance was threatened by Ruth, his newly discovered half-sister?

Whichever way she turned, Ruth met dark Tregellas eyes, always carefully veiling their innermost thoughts; even her father's manner was strange, evading discussion of her past, unwilling to help her recover her lost memory.

So, with the carved dragons looming larger and larger in her thoughts, Ruth tried desperately to work out who wanted her dead, before it was too late.

Barbara Banks

Dragonseeds

ST. MARTIN'S PRESS
NEW YORK

ROBERT HALE LIMITED
LONDON

St. Martin's Press, Inc.
175 Fifth Avenue,
New York, N.Y. 10010.

Library of Congress Catalog Card Number 76-29854

ISBN 0-312-21927-X

First published in Great Britain 1977

ISBN 0 7091 6098 4

Robert Hale Limited
Clerkenwell House
Clerkenwell Green
London EC1R oHT

Printed in Great Britain by
Clarke, Doble & Brendon Ltd,
Plymouth and London

ONE

The coach lurched to a noisy stop, recalling me abruptly to my surroundings just in time to save the letters sliding from my knee. Crumpling them quickly, but safely, in one hand I stood up and reached my case from the overhead rack with my free hand, then joined my fellow passengers in jostling towards the exit.

My stomach twitched with apprehension as I descended the steps. In a few minutes I could be involved in an unpleasant argument. But all I had to do, I told myself, was stand by my former decision and return the money. Nothing more.

Skirting the rear of the coach I realised I was purposely dawdling. "Come on, Ruth, don't be a coward!" I said under my breath and stepped determinedly free of the coach's last stragglers.

I heard the car's engine before I looked up, but the blueness was almost on me. My cry, as I backed and fell, was drowned by the sound of the car and I hardly felt pain as it hit me. Faces were hanging over me, stifling me. I pushed my hands upwards to clear them away and they blurred and then disappeared into nothing.

I'd been conscious for some time, but drowsy, unable to sort out my thoughts. Now, I opened my eyes fully and gradually the blackness dissolved and a ceiling came into focus. Elongated shadows chased over its surface, thrown by a tree outside a large window. I let my eyes follow the shadows downwards to a tubular bedrail with a chart, complete with a fat, bulldog clip and then I recognised the

7

pungent smell.

"Hospital!" I said aloud.

"Yes, Miss Tregellas!" The nurse had appeared quietly.

Strange how large, round people were often so light on their feet, with easy smiling faces that you couldn't help responding to. But my smile changed to a grimace at the bitterness in my mouth.

"Dry, are you?" She was sympathetic, pouring water into a glass, then raising and propping me against my pillows. "Only a little sip for now!"

Obediently, I sipped. The water, like iced silk, slithered onto my parched tongue. I let it lie a moment at the back of my throat, enjoying it, then gulped it down quickly.

Tregellas, the nurse had said—Miss Tregellas. I turned the name over in my mind but it remained unfamiliar, unattached to me, and the thinking merely emphasised a headache that started at the back of my ears and worked its way outwards from there.

"Am I ill?"

If my nurse thought the words odd, she didn't let it show, as she answered me: "Nothing serious!" and would have added more, but the click of the door opening interrupted her and she said instead, "Miss Tregellas is fully conscious now, Doctor."

Conscious, but not thinking very clearly and certainly not seeing well, I decided, blinking up at the ruddy face that hung over me. He had moved across the room and blotted out my upward view before I'd had time to adjust to another presence. More like a farmer than a Doctor surely, and would that moustache fit under a surgical mask?

". . . Doctor, Miss Tregellas."

I collected my drifting thoughts to ask: "What is wrong with me, Doctor?"

"Slight concussion, nothing more." His voice was controlled and professional. "There are a few stitches here." His fingers explored my head gently. "You should be leaving us tomorrow or the next day. Rest is all that's necessary,

8

though you may feel a little weak at first."

"But what happened to me?" I persisted. "I don't recall any accident!"

"You were jay-walking."

"Jay-walking!"

"From behind a coach in Galston, yesterday. Straight into the path of a car coming the opposite way. You're lucky to be alive, Miss Tregellas."

The slightly stilted words suggested that anyone irresponsible enough to step in front of a car deserved concussion, and I was stung to reply: "I don't suppose I did it on purpose and anyway, I can't remember a thing."

He frowned. "Temporary amnesia. Quite common. By tomorrow you'll probably have recovered sufficiently to fill in all the minor details connected with the unfortunate incident. If not, your father can. He had the misfortune to arrive almost immediately after it happened."

He peered in my eyes, glanced at my chart, gave me a brisk 'good-day' and was gone.

I waited until the sound of his footsteps was fading before asking: "Is he always like that?"

"Been like that as long as I've known him," her uniformed shoulders shrugged. "It's just his way, he's soft enough underneath and as honest as they come. Expects everyone else to live up to his standards too. But forget him and think about your father's visit this evening."

"What time is it?"

"Now? Just gone one. You missed lunch, but tea's at four. Rest until then, it'll do you good."

I was tired. Even lying in bed I felt exhausted and there was something I wanted to think about too. What was it? I let myself relax completely while the nurse—Nurse Tulk according to the oblong badge pinned to her uniform—tucked and patted the bed tidy. Sure enough the niggling worry returned. It was Tregellas! Eyes closed, I spelt it out ... T-R-E-G-E-L-L-A-S ... once ... twice ... then the letters were revolving and sleep was overtaking me. Fatalistically,

9

I gave in. Later, I would figure it out.

I flexed and arched my body tentively, careful not to jolt my head. No ill-effects, so I continued with the exercise; fingers and toes, a wriggle; arms and legs, a stretch. A few small bruises, plus a large one on my thigh, I discovered, but the overall feeling was good.

"You're looking better," Nurse Tulk said cheerfully. "All coming back is it?"

"No, it isn't. But I've only just woken up," I said slowly, wondering if it would be better to let my missing memory work its own way back or try bombarding it with questions to hurry the process.

"Well, see if this helps."

This, was a large black handbag, dropped on the bed.

"It looks new, doesn't it?" I said, fingering the soft leather and liking the king-sized bronze buckle that served as fastening and decoration.

I made a well by draping the sheet over my knees, then up-ended the bag's contents. Nothing struck an immediate cord. Not the handkerchief, nor the shiny floral cosmetic bag. I unzipped the small bag and tipped the lipsticks and varied containers into my well. There were three lipsticks; two pinky shades and the third a cool orange. Tweezers, face powder, eye make-up; the things an average girl would carry with her. I drew a little zigzag on the back of my hand with the orange lipstick. When I smudged it with my forefinger it gave off a faint perfume.

"Perfume," I said. "Perfume, I know I saw some here . . ."

"Got it." Nurse Tulk sat herself comfortably near my knees, her ample figure denting the mattress and rolling the perfume and other items down to her.

It was a slim twisted phial, cool and familiar in my fingers. The peaked stopper screwed off easily so that in a moment I had it to my nose, sniffing, my eyes shut to appreciate the fragrance more completely. In the corridors of my mind something stirred and I knew this was definitely my perfume, chosen by me.

If I rest quietly, without moving, this scent could be the key, I told myself, trying not to encroach on the whisperings in my head. I shook the bottle, encouraging the spiciness to rise again. Words and pictures hovered uncertainly as I sought to grasp and identify the perfumed thoughts, then, on the verge of . . . what? . . . a door slammed close by and it all slid away.

"Gone, I'm afraid," my eyes opened to meet the questioning gaze of Nurse Tulk.

"Look through the other things," she advised. "They may mean something to you."

Aspirins, scissors and a combined wallet-purse. A few coins rattled in the purse side, but I was more interested in the thickness of the wallet compartment. The notes were all new, fresh from the bank, for the numbers followed each other from the bottom to the top of the fat, neat, wad. I pulled them far enough out to roughly check the numbers and convince myself that I was fairly well off. Then, with Nurse Tulk's inquisitive eyes on me, I fastened the strap of the wallet and dropped it beside the floral bag.

For such a large attractive handbag its contents were most disappointing. A small notebook, with a spiral top to turn its pages on, had nothing of interest in it, page after page of blankness, until I came to the cardboard base. There in the middle were five figures—27821. I circled the number slowly, with a pencil from the bed. A phone number perhaps?

"Well, not much there." I was suddenly depressed as well as stiff. Straightening my knees I collapsed my sheet, rustling a folded piece of paper under the edge of the handbag. A letter—without an envelope. As I picked it up small flecks of dried mud flaked from it.

"Oh yes, I forgot about that,' Nurse Tulk tutted. "Apparently you dropped it when you were knocked down. You must've been reading it when the coach stopped. I expect you picked up your suitcase and kept the letter in your hand. I guess someone put it in your handbag for you after the accident. Good of them!"

"Very good!" I agreed, my mind darting away on this new theme. So I'd been on the coach had I? Coming to Galston, and with a suitcase. Funny, I'd never thought of myself getting off the coach, only of stepping from behind it.

The letter shook in my fingers as I opened it and flattened the cream paper hard against my knees.

Dragonseeds!

The gold embossing, hard under my fingertips, projected the word at my startled eyes, while my brain reasoned that this was the name of a house. A date, written in erratic, cramped letters, was some weeks before, I saw, checking with the calendar on the wall.

Dear Daughter,

I can hardly believe you are coming to me at Dragonseeds. I've told my Father, your Grandfather Justin, everything that was said when last I met you and he is excitedly looking forward to your arrival.

To think that if my Father had not insisted on another advertisement in *The Times*, after all these years, I would never have found you . . .

the 'and' was almost non-existent where a corner had been torn off the bottom of the page. Impatiently, I turned to the back of the sheet. It was bare and there was no second sheet to the letter.

Damnation! To have my curiosity raised to such a pitch and then chopped off. The writing might be small, leaning first one way and then the other, but the writer didn't believe in putting more than half a dozen words on one line before leaving a large space and starting a new line.

I rubbed the hard golden word at the head of the letter. "Dragonseeds!" I didn't realise that I had spoken aloud until I was answered.

"Yes, you'll be home there soon. Maybe tomorrow."

"Into the unknown!" I said dramatically, waving my arms, but my voice wobbled. So I stopped pretending. "Nurse, tell me about Dragonseeds and my father . . .

please! You don't know what a fool I feel, how helpless, just having a void instead of people to remember and conversations and . . . and, oh, everything like that." A thought struck me: "You do know Dragonseeds, don't you?"

"Know it!" She laughed. "I should think I do. Everyone in these parts does. And the Tregellas family." She paused and her face was lit with renewed interest. "But then, I forgot, you're what the Galston Evening News called the long lost member of the family." She laughed again. "Fancy me telling you about your own folks."

"Me? Long lost?" This new facet of my problems shook me. "What d'you mean? What did the papers say? Tell me!" My voice, I knew, was rising.

"Sssh! You're all flushed. Doctor'll be after me if you get too excited. Will you lie quiet if I tell you a few bits. Just enough to help jog your memory along."

Poor Nurse Tulk; gossip and nurse were conflicting within her, plus an emotion I couldn't pinpoint; embarrassment? But I was selfishly concerned with my own feelings, and I waved her on impatiently.

"Well, the papers said you were born after your mother and father parted. They didn't say she ran away, but it's common knowledge she did. So he never knew—your father —whether he'd a son or a daughter, poor man. He had masses of enquiries made, so they say, but your mother'd disappeared completely. It was your Grandfather, old Justin Tregellas, that started the whole thing up again. He got your father to advertise, in *The Times* it was, to try and trace you both. You must've seen it and now you're going to live at Dragonseeds."

She'd recited the news parrot-fashion, but with enjoyment, starting slowly and finishing, out of breath, with a triumphant rush.

"And . . . my mother?"

"Dead!" Her eyes fell away from mine and I knew I'd correctly read that earlier emotion as embarrassment.

So the erratic writing was my father's. I touched the word blazoned at the top of the paper. If Dragonseeds was to be my home, the Tregellas family, my family, then I must know more of them. It would be hard to imagine a more impossible situation. Here I lay, a 'long lost member of the family', to quote Nurse Tulk, with the added drawback of a memory that was one large hole.

I hoped, fervently, that Doctor Byford was right and that soon it would be possible for me to fill in all those missing blocks of nothingness.

It appeared to be Grandfather who was mainly responsible for me being restored to the family. Grandfather Tregellas. It was unnerving to find I could not bring to mind one small detail of this man who was so altering my life. Yet I must have discussed the family with my father; have been told, if ever so briefly, of Grandfather Tregellas and others of the Tregellas clan at Dragonseeds. And Father? I couldn't even dredge up the colour of his eyes. Doctor Byford and his 'temporary amnesia—quite common', I brooded.

Maybe it was lying back against the pillow's coolness and letting my annoyance with Doctor Byford sweep over me that encouraged the first of my remembering. Though why the Doctor's ruddy features should have that effect, I didn't know. But it started—mistily—an indistinct, faceless thought; not a mind picture, but a mind thought; a man in a wheelchair—Grandfather, I was convinced.

"Is my Grandfather confined to a wheelchair?"

Nurse Tulk's face confirmed it before she said, "Yes, but how did you know?"

"I just did!" I said, terrifically elated by this tiny breakthrough. "The Doctor was right, it's starting to come back."

"Good, you'll just about have time to remember your accident, your father and the family tree before visiting time."

For a second I thought she meant it, until she laughed. Father, she said, would be visiting me after tea.

The tea tray came and went. I was in a turmoil. What

should I say to him? A father only recently met after a lifetime apart and then not to recall our meeting.

"Well, one thing you'll be able to talk about," said Nurse Tulk, pushing the door open with her solid rear, "is flowers," and she panted in, hardly visible behind an armful of great sprays of mimosa and daffodils. Like Spring entering the room in a cloud of yellow. 'I hope you are feeling better. Father.' said the same spidery writing as in my letter.

I rested until the visiting bell then suddenly felt panic. Quickly, I found lipstick and mirror—to help boost my morale. I held the glass high for the best light and then froze.

None of my bewilderment was mirrored in the dark eyes that met mine; thickly fringed lashes touched my cheek-bones as I blinked and ran a finger along my winged brows. This face, with little change, had belonged to me for twenty odd years? Certainly the hair would not normally be snatched back in a bandage hairband, away from the stitched bump; but this small featured girl with the pale skin was me.

I applied the colour but wished that I'd left the stranger in the mirror until later. A rap on the door startled me, I dropped the lipstick, and Nurse Tulk opened the door. This, I knew would be Father.

He took a short step towards me then stood, looking and waiting, I felt, for me to speak first. Self-conscious, I blurted out; "Goodness, aren't we alike!"

His features relaxed and he moved towards me smiling. Nurse Tulk beamed at us both, then left.

There was a tiny pause, then he said carefully: "I'm relieved you've woken up. I've been worried."

"Stupid thing to do, walk into a car. Doctor Byford was very scathing."

He wasn't listening to me, I saw. He said: "You won't let this change things, will you?" And his face, taut with concern, bent over me, so that I was able to see that what I had taken for a resemblance at first sight wasn't in fact so.

It was the eyes that had misled me, with their irises

almost lost in the darkness encircling them, but in a skin of maple brown, whereas my hands were honeypale against the sheets.

"Change things?" I echoed and was glad I had not inherited the trait of sticking out my jaw so aggressively. At least, I didn't think I ever did it. I should have to watch myself.

"Coming to Dragonseeds! You promised you would come! Everything is arranged, as we planned! Everything! You remember?" His voice was unsteady and a vein throbbed in his temple; one hand started to smooth his hair then instead scraped it forward with an impatient, disarranging movement.

It meant so much to him. I felt a flood of warmth for this man, laying bare his own feelings. It was obvious that the most important thing in his life was that I should live at Dragonseeds; be with him. Being wanted was a beautiful, exhilarating, wonderful experience.

"Of course I'm returning with you, Father. Whatever made you think I should change my mind?" I did have a twinge of guilt as I spoke the words, knowing I could remember nothing of the original promise. It was the guilt, I think, that made me lean impulsively across the bed to touch his hand. Then, I drew him down to sit on the edge of the bed. I was searching, vainly, for the right words to break to him that, though he was my father, I could remember nothing of any former meeting or meetings—that he was a complete stranger to me.

No fluent, soothing words came, so instead I said, without finesse: "Father, I've lost my memory!"

His re-actions were swift, chasing across his face; incredulity, then a frown that clenched his eyebrows together in twin clefts above his nose.

I was watching nervously but still unprepared for the involuntary tightening of his fingers on mine. My "Ouch!" came out on a gasp as I tried to release my hand.

"What do you mean? Lost your memory? You can't

16

have!"

My lately found sense of well-being was gone as I insisted, "But I have! It's not my fault, Father! I know it's a shock to you. It was to me. It still is. But I've started to remember again. I knew Grandfather was in a wheelchair. Doctor Byford said it will all come back eventually and I'm not to worry . . . So don't you worry . . . please!"

As suddenly as the harsh lines had appeared, so they were ironed out, leaving his face bland, smiling. The hand that had ruffled his dark hair earlier now shaped it tidily back while I felt my bruised fingers patted reassuringly.

He stayed another ten minutes explaining how he'd never forgive himself for not being at the coach stop to meet me the previous day. I don't suppose it would have made a scrap of difference, I comforted; but he was determined to make himself responsible for the accident, so I let him. He was rapping his watch with two well shaped fingernails, transferring a portion of the blame for yesterday's lateness to it, for being slow.

"Yes," I said listlessly, feeling as though all the sand had run out of me.

The watch thumping stopped and his gaze transferred from his wrist to me. "I'm sorry, you're tired. Tomorrow afternoon I'll take you home—to Dragonseeds. You're not to concern yourself with anything. I'll make all the arrangements with Doctor Byford and see to your luggage." He hesitated, "I shouldn't try to force your memory. Leave it to return naturally." His hands rested briefly on my shoulders as he kissed me on the cheek, before leaving with a cheerful wave.

Peace at last. I slithered down the bed and allowed myself to think of tomorrow. Dragonseeds was conjuring in me an excitement that bordered on fear. I'd ask Nurse Tulk to tell me more of what she knew of my relations and home to be. Grandfather would be there to meet me, and who else? Yes, I needed help. How many people inhabited Dragonseeds? What did the oddly named house look like?

I could visualise a flight of steps to the main door. Once inside Father would say: 'This is your Grandfather Tregellas' and he would turn to the man in the wheelchair, saying, 'Father, this is your Grand-daughter . . .' My mind faltered and the image of tomorrow faded. I tried the words again, this time out loud, straight at the calendar on the wall. 'Father, this is your Grand-daughter . . .'

"My God!" I scrambled frantically in my mind, searching. I laughed and it shrilled in the newly arrived twilight of the room. It couldn't happen—but it had. How had my Father, rather primly, opened his letter to me? 'Dear Daughter', and how had he addressed me this very afternoon? I rehashed our conversation, word by word. What I sought was not there.

"I don't know my name! My own name!" I told the calendar, trying to suppress the bubbles of hysteria rising in me.

Did all amnesia victims feel this final shattering of the calm and experience the odd sensation that the very shadows contained life!

I hadn't heard the click of the door, but now I knew that the greyness cloaking the door did contain movement, for a voice of chilling clarity, yet with undertones of mockery said:

"Your name? Why your name is Ruth . . . little cousin!"

TWO

"He'd no business calling on you! What did he say?" My Father's voice was stiff with anger, his knuckles white on the wheel.

I muffled a sigh. The departure from the Nursing Home, Nurse Tulk wrapping me firmly in a travelling rug in the passenger seat, then Father anchoring me with the safety belt had all run so smoothly; even Doctor Byford had managed an enigmatic smile, a half wave. I had watched the two figures grow smaller as we drove away from the building, climbing almost immediately to where the short drive led on to a cliff road.

Below us was the sprawling town of Galston, a rich mixture of old and new, from its grey harbour, clustered with small cottages and warehouses, to the confetti of colour provided by visitors who had come and seen and, finally, built their stucco bungalows.

Now we were ascending, steeply, and the town was blotted out. I'd be enjoying this, I thought with some resentment, if it weren't for Father. So it was that I sighed and answered: "He only stayed a few minutes. He called me his little cousin, Ruth."

In telling it to my Father I relived that few minutes when Dominic had stepped from the shadows.

"What d'you want in here? Who are you?" I'd called out, and I think I'd also added that I would scream if he came a step nearer—just like a heroine in an old fashioned melodrama.

"Surely Uncle Fabian has spoken of me? Your cousin, Dominic!" And when I pressed myself hard into the pillows: "You're not frightened of me, are you, little cousin?"

Temper, a rush of adrenalin, enabled me to sit bolt upright and tell him loudly that he must leave. I don't think that normally a command from a small girl in the middle of a rumpled bed would have carried much weight with cousin Dominic, but I was suddenly re-inforced by Nurse Tulk. Light flooded the room and I saw Dominic Tregellas clearly for the first time.

He seemed extremely tall from where I sat, head and shoulders above my stumpy nurse, who was making vague shooing noises at this uninvited visitor. But it was obvious that she recognised him as a Tregellas and the shooing was not as definite as I would have liked it to be.

He managed to delay his departure long enough to say, silkily, that it would have been unforgivable to pass so close to the Home without calling on his long lost cousin. And green flecks in his eyes, glinted with sly malice and the 'long lost' was faintly emphasised.

"Did you tell him about your amnesia?" Father queried sharply.

"I had to," I pointed out. "He knew something was wrong from the first. Anyway, it would be impossible for me to talk to any of the family for long without them spotting I wasn't," I hesitated, "myself."

I was reluctant to divulge that Dominic had supplied me with my own name. The smile that had accompanied the information, sensed rather than seen, the mockery underlying the words, had been hateful, and I kept a too detailed description of Dominic's manner to myself, hoping to ease the tension that filled the car. It was ironic, for by watering down the account of my cousin's visit I was, in a way, defending him, whereas, basing my feelings on our initial encounter, I felt a strong antagonism for the handsome man with his biting tongue.

Through the window the Cornish scenery rushed by; hills then moorland, patterned with touches of yellow. Damp,

20

mossy scents mixed with unknown fragrances, filtered in the partly opened side window. They would be from the golden wimbushes and the primroses tucked in the valleys, according to Nurse Tulk. She had spent as much of the morning as she could spare from her duties, describing the surrounding countryside; the granite castles that had once stood as dour guardians of this coast, with its caves, its incredible rock piles and the dozens of Coves with strange names; Emerald Cove, Merlin's Cove, the Cove of the Red Stones.

Finally, I had learnt a little more of the House of Tregellas. Titbits of information that I stored like a magpie.

"Well, who lives at Dragonseeds, besides Grandfather Tregellas and Father?" I had asked.

Surprisingly, my informant's usually active tongue had dawdled over answering. Her, "Weeell . . ." had marked time, before she said: "There's your cousin, Dominic, of course. He does most of the running of the Estate, along with your Father, for old Mr. Tregellas. Then there's Hannah."

"Hannah Tregellas!"

"No, no, Hannah's not family . . . though she is in a way. She's always been there, ever since she went as nursemaid to the twins."

"Twins?" I echoed.

"Your Father, Fabian, and his twin, Marcus. Hannah raised them, then stayed on. You could say Hannah was family really."

So Father was a twin. Did Marcus share the same mercurial temperament? Did his writing lean to the left then the right?

"So counting Father, there are, let me see," I tapped my fingers, "one . . . two . . . three . . . four people, and I'll make the fifth. Or are there any staff living in?"

No staff living in, Nurse Tulk replied vaguely. There were estate workers, gardeners, cleaners and a maid living within walking distance, but Hannah shouldered the responsibility of running the house apparently.

Poor Hannah, her position evolving over the years from nursemaid, spoon-feeding and nappy changing, to a sort of female Atlas, finally. Quite a task for one woman who would be, I surmised, approximately twenty years older than Father.

"All that thinking of meals and cleaning, arranging. However does Hannah cope, at her age?" I asked indignantly on the unknown Hannah's behalf.

"She does get some help, don't forget," Nurse Tulk pointed out. "I told you the big cleaning jobs are seen to and . . . well, she doesn't have to do all the worrying herself." And to my surprise my usually talkative Nurse was at the door and gone.

These fragments that were part of my lifeline, were in my thoughts as I stared, unseeing, through the car window.

"We're an old established family in these parts, aren't we Father?"

For a moment he turned to me and I saw his face, bare and free of the nagging V between his brows, the cloudy curtain in his eyes. Pride smoothed his face with youth for the seconds he faced me, then once more he was frowning with concentration, giving his full attention to following the road where it struck upwards, northwards.

"The Tregellas are *the* family in these parts; we've been here since Norman times. But it was the fifteenth century before we were strong enough and wealthy enough to erect our first fortress—Dinas-Du."

"Black Castle," I said.

"Yes, yes, that's right." His tone altered slightly. "You're remembering it seems."

"Not consciously," I felt forced to admit, "But when you said Dinas-Du, I said Black Castle without thinking. Anyway, go on."

"I can't tell you much more in the little time we've left before we reach Dragonseeds. Look! . . . when we turn again—the trees are obstructing our view at the moment—

22

you will see my . . . our home. After that it's only a little way."

Until now the last weak sunshine of the day had spread pale light over the landscape, suddenly it was gone and dark clouds rode across the steep skyline.

I shivered in the rug and without turning to me Father closed the side window nearest to him. It seemed pointless to mention that I was not cold, that the shiver had been of the kind one would experience sitting in the dark listening to ghost stories. Mentally shaking myself I resumed listening to Father and the history of Dinas-Du.

"It was destroyed almost completely—Black Castle—by the Spaniards. They appeared one morning in 1595, in their galleons, and caught us unawares." His voice was intense, as though he was speaking of an event in which he'd taken part. "The village below us, Gwellan, was almost wiped out too. It was only the Tregellas rallying the remaining villagers together with the fishermen from the nearby Coves, that repulsed the Spaniards finally."

"We're a tough lot." I found I was laughing.

"We are," Father agreed, laughing with me. "But it was my Grandfather Adam Tregellas who restored the family and its fortunes at a much later date. Black Adam they called him. There's Spanish blood in the family, I suspect. So with a touch of Spanish blood mixed with the blood of Pink . . ."

"Pink Pearl," I finished. "The Bride from the East."

It was a strange sensation, having these snippets of information spring to my lips before I even had time to know they were there. There had been my strange mind picture of Grandfather Tregellas in his wheelchair and since then the words Black Castle and Pink Pearl that had been spoken as though by another person. How soon would the patchwork pieces of my memory tie up into one whole past so that I could shake off the feeling of being two people.

"Pink Pearl really was a pearl among women." Father was continuing; "She was fifteen years old to Adam's fifty

23

nine when he brought her back aboard his clipper, together
with silks and jade."

"Spring and Winter! Did it work?"

"Admirably, for two years, by which time my father,
Justin Tregellas, was born. Then Pink Pearl caught a chill
that developed into pneumonia. She was dead in a few
hours."

"Poor Adam," I said softly.

"Oh, he certainly lost his roar after she died. But he had
his fortune made by this time and an heir. Instead of sitting
down and pining he set to work on the building of a shrine
to her memory, on the ruins of Black Castle."

"Dragonseeds!"

We were silent a while, thinking our own thoughts.
Darkness enclosed us except for the car's headlights, fighting gloom and drizzle, the cavernous overhand of the hill,
still striving upwards.

It could only be minutes till we reached our destination.

"Who will be at Dragonseeds?" Did the quiver in my
voice tell Father of my inner turmoil? I hoped so.

The pause before he answered me seemed to be caused by
the extra attention he was giving to the twists and turns of
the road. I knew this, yet felt edgy at the slowness of his
reply.

"Family," he said at last.

"Grandfather Justin," I prompted. The one who holds the
purse strings was how Nurse Tulk had described him.

"And Dominic." Ill-humour flared up; the recollection of
his nephew's informal visit to me at the Home still a sore
point. But only momentarily; a softer emotion replaced it.
"He's Marcus's son. My brother, Marcus. I . . . I still miss him,
though it's twenty years since he died." The last words
were squeezed out. "His wife drowned with him. In the
river that runs through the bottom fields, where it turns
round Gwellan."

So Marcus was dead. I should never have the opportunity
to compare his character with that of my Father, his twin,

except through memories stored by the family. But memories are fickle and coloured by later events, not to mention the opinions of the brain they're secreted in.

"Who brought Dominic up? Mother?" I asked, for something to say, because my own lack of any memories was niggling at me again, and also I wanted to divert Father's thoughts from his dead brother. That Dominic would have been a very young boy when my mother ran away was a fact that hadn't really struck me until I realised that I had triggered off yet another awkward pause.

"Hannah raised Dominic. You'll meet her soon," he answered shortly.

I wanted to ask more questions—quickly—to fill up mountains of emptiness on matters that were suddenly vital. But I remained speechless. How much of the Tregellas family history had mother told me, I wondered. And how much had been supplied by Father at our meeting in London; he had mentioned London casually as the location of our first re-union when speaking of another matter. I wished now that I had followed it up. It made no difference to the outcome, for the time being I remembered nothing of what either of my parents had told me. Nurse Tulk had been a mine of information, but it was hard to define where gossip and true facts merged.

The car swung sharply, then straightened out, still below the hill that had overlooked us earlier, but at a more acute angle. Now, facing where the last of the sun had shown itself, a streak of biege sky lingered, with the remains of the cliff-end superimposed upon it. Rolling away from the harsh edge, coming inland, the hill smoothed out before falling away to form a great humped mass of land. But it was the shape crouched along the back of the headland that drew my eyes; it hovered blackly like some savage beast eager to leap and devour its prey.

"Dragonseeds!" said Father, unnecessarily.

I released myself from the safety belt and as Father came round and opened the door I inhaled a breath of the damp, raw air that bit into the car's stuffy interior.

Light fanned from a door in the centre of two great
pillars, creating slats of black and white down a flight of
steps.

"They've heard the car," said Father.

"Yes," I answered, surprised to find myself so weary and
uncertain that no further words came.

The few yards to the door on Father's arm I found un-
pleasantly wobbly. I was glad of the astringent iciness of
the drizzle laden air slapping on my skin, freshening me,
so that I managed the last few steps to the studded doors on
my own.

The brightness that met us as we left the cold night and
entered Dragonseeds made my eyes water. I stood, rubbing
my arm where a metal stud had grazed it as I stumbled in.
The hollow throb of the great doors behind us emphasised
my quickened heartbeat.

"Thank you, Symon," Father said to someone behind us,
then to me: "Come right through, Ruth, to the Library.
You can rest in one of the big chairs and Hannah will bring
you a drink."

My heels drew staccato clicks from the mosaic floor.
Looking down I saw I was progressing along the tail of a
great dragon, via its scales and claws until, at an alcoved
doorway that obviously led to the Library, I was treading
the fiery breath issuing from its flared nostrils.

A murmur of voices seeped from behind a lacquer screen
that was half concealing the entrance to the room. As I
reached the screen I took a deep breath to fortify myself
to meet Dominic and . . . who else?

I stood close beside Father, a little to the rear of him, blinking in the brilliance cast by teak coloured dragons hanging
from above. The dark bodies were a blur beyond their serrated
heads, but light spewed from the gaping jaws in a cunning
and effective manner, so that when I looked away from
them and tried to make out the occupants of the chairs, I
saw instead distorted bodies with electrified heads.

26

My family really are dragons, I thought, and choked back an overwhelming need to laugh.

"Ruth," said Father, leading me by the hand, "this is your Grandfather."

The false images that filled my vision faded and I was facing a wheelchair and Justin Tregellas. The hand he thrust at me was bird-like, a network of veins, yet it was vitally alive clasped in my fingers. He would have overflowed the chair forty years before, I guessed, now he was lost in the folds of a blanket and cushions. Only the ageless eyes manœuvred easily.

"Welcome to Dragonseeds, my dear," he said at last, releasing my hand and turning his attention from me to the man in the chair next to him.

It was Dominic, and as I forced my eyes to meet his he was rising to his feet to present a small bow and a twisted smile that, I knew, went no further than his lips.

"You've met Dominic, I believe," Grandfather said.

"Yes," I agreed, hardly audible above Dominic's explanation to Grandfather, for the second time, no doubt, that it would have been the height of bad manners not to have made the acquaintance of his long lost cousin when he was passing the Nursing Home. Listening, I recalled those first words from him; 'Your name? Why your name is Ruth . . . little cousin,' and I felt hot again, and prickly with temper and tiredness.

It was demoralising to find someone disliked you and let it show. It was worse when that person was possessed of a strong personality allied to exceptional good looks. Under ordinary circumstances, I would probably have been attracted to cousin Dominic. As it was, all I felt was a growing dislike that verged on hatred and apprehension at the frightening emotions that had grown in so short a period of time.

"Fabian, introduce the others," Grandfather ordered and my Father guided me towards another leather chair.

The woman was knitting. I realised I'd been aware of the

sound ever since entering the Library. It had continued softly, like the pit-pat of tiny feet, unhesitating, as background to the brief conversations between Grandfather, Dominic and myself. Now she abandoned the knitting, halfway along the row, pushing the stitches safely to the end of the needles, folding the garment so that the needles lay parallel with each other, before impaling the yellow ball of wool on the points, with careful deliberation.

My Father's fingers under my elbow were over tight as he said: "This is Bella, Ruth . . ." And as he hesitated, she finished, ". . . his wife. I'm your step-mother. I hope you don't mind!"

I drew a quick breath, then put my hand to my mouth and changed it to a cough before I bent down to the figure wedged comfortably in the chair. Did she know, and not care, that her red dress matched the upholstery, so that her body provided a middle hillock between the chair's arms.

Our hands met. My cold one warmed in her fleshy fingers, then gently freed.

"I'm sure Fabian didn't tell you," she continued, her husky voice rising from way down inside her. And there was sympathy and laughter mixed in her placid face, in her almost black eyes.

"Tut, tut, Uncle Fabian! Fancy forgetting to tell Ruth of your new wife, your brave effort to start anew and wipe out the past. And now Ruth is here from the past, Uncle Fabian."

I could have struck Dominic, but I didn't even turn towards him; feeling his hostility like a web around me, his eyes making a cold spot, like ice, between my shoulder blades.

I hadn't answered Bella, but Grandfather's reedy tones forestalled me; "Never mind the past, Dominic. For the moment at any rate. And you, Fabian, call Hannah and see Ruth gets a warm drink, and for goodness sake introduce the others."

Whoever had opened then slammed the main doors when

28

Father and I had arrived was hovering at the back of us still. Several times I had part turned to see who it was, but then my attention had been channeled forward again by an introduction. I remembered Father saying, 'Thank you, Symon,' and then I had walked along the dragon's tail and his flaming breath and into the Dragon family.

So I turned at last to get my first sight of Symon, while Father called, 'Hannah' loudly at a door higher up the room. He was standing quite still, a boy of perhaps ten years, with the look of a Tregellas about him.

"My son, Symon," Bella said, as Father returned.

"Hello Symon," I said, knowing they were watching me, as I tried to accept calmly that this, presumably, made Symon my half-brother. As he made no move towards me and his face remained impassive, unwelcoming, I didn't risk a rebuff by offering my hand.

The needles resumed their clicking and Father hurried me between chairs past the arrogant Dominic, shoulders resting casually against a row of thick volumes spattered with gold lettering. With me came Grandfather, twiddling the dials on one arm of his wheelchair, causing it to move smoothly forward with a low hum, like drowsy bees.

"Watch out for your feet, cousin," drawled Dominic. "Grandfather's notorious for not caring whose feet he runs over."

A grunt was Grandfather's only acknowledgement, but I moved away from the humming contraption, noticing for the first time that a good deal of the furniture was scored as though with a knife.

We progressed in a small convoy to the far end of the Library, hemmed in by towering shelves of leather bound mustiness, until a young man barred our way. He stood, smiling, a finger marking the place in his book. I didn't need to be told he was related to Bella; the same serenely pleasant face looked down into mine, but where Bella's true features were blurred in folds of flesh, this man's bone structure was clear cut, well shaped. His smile was quick, reaching his eyes, and after Symon's blank face and Dominic's twitch of the mouth that passed for a smile, I was ready to cry with relief for a touch of warmth from someone.

I was saying, "How do you do!" and holding out my hand to him before Father could say, "This is Neal Pendeen, Bella's brother."

"May I add my welcome to Dragonseeds."

"Thank you . . ." I hesitated, "Neal."

His other hand closed over mine and I let it lie, thinking that this was the only truly happy moment I could recall.

Father and Neal, between them, settled me in a deep red chair, alongside Bella and her unravelling ball of yellow. Symon had disappeared, Grandfather was crossing verbal swords with Dominic. The thin voice rose and fell in a switchback of sound, while the harsher tones of my cousin persisted evenly until only his voice remained.

"You'll get used to them," Bella said. "Sometimes it's the daffodils or the serpentine or even a fly on the wall. They'll find something to argue over."

"Is it ever serious?" I asked her, straining my ears for any resumption of the discord.

"I don't think so," Bella's free knitting pin was serving as a back-scratcher, the knob twitching between her shoulder blades, and I watched with fascination the look of bliss that dulled her eyes. To my amazement her lids drooped, quivered, then settled firmly. She inhaled, breathed out slowly and was asleep.

"Your drink. It'll do you good." I hadn't heard Hannah come and it was easy to see why. She was an adult in miniature, from the pad of mousy hair piled on top of her head, in a vain attempt to add inches, down to her tiny feet encased in sheepskin shoes.

I heard Dominic approaching. Though I wasn't accustomed to the sound of his footsteps I knew the self-assured tread could only belong to him.

"This is our very own Hannah," he said, his arm encircling the bird-like figure, raising it so that the sheepskin slippers were practically on their tiptoes and the drink rocked unsteadily.

"Put me down this instant." A slap accompanied the command and for the first time I heard genuine laughter from Dominic. Devilment lifted his thick brows to an incredible angle over eyes that glinted wickedly, and the smile that curled his lips softened his whole face.

I said, "Thank you," and "Hello Hannah," and rescued my drink simultaneously.

Hannah acknowledged Dominic's introduction and then told me firmly: "Your room's ready for you if you feel like going up after your drink."

The drink was scalding; milk with a lavish helping of honey stirred in.

Lord! but I was tired. Perhaps the drink had supplied the final knock out. I slid my tongue across my lips to gather in the dregs of stickiness and told Hannah: "Yes, please, I will go up. I'm terribly tired."

I hardly noticed the route I took to my bedroom. I remember the eyes as I left the Library. Even Bella's heavy lids were raised and all-seeing. Only Neal's glance seemed to contain warmth and understanding—like his handshake— as he wished me 'goodnight'. Symon's eyes I felt rather than saw. A movement behind the lacquer screen betrayed where he stood.

Experiencing a sharp resentment, I addressed a 'goodnight' to the screen, but Symon remained silent and the spite drained from me.

Grandfather Tregellas's chair followed me to the foot of the stairs, where the wide shallow steps rose from the claws of the mosaic dragon I'd trod earlier. Only half aware of the intricately wrought, white bannisters that supported me up the endless stairs, I was thankful when Hannah threw open a door, the second on the left of the landing.

I was alone at last. Free to let down my defences and be me, weary and lonely, with a head full of questions and tears on my cheeks.

The bed was plump and inviting, placed in the centre of the wall opposite the door. I liked the cool columbine and white of its cover and the headrest fixed to the wall with buttons forming rounds and dips that would be very comfortable to a head as heavy as mine. Sitting on the edge to test it, led to kicking off my shoes, and so to lying back and closing my eyes. I remember thinking I shouldn't be resting on top of the bed, it might mar its freshness—then I was asleep.

I had turned on my side, knees tucked up high, so that when a small sound in the house awakened me, my vision was filled by an imposing fireplace fashioned in blocks of rough pink granite. In place of hot coals, its well was filled with long branches, heavy with soft rosy blossom, spilling from a bronze urn. I rolled over on my back to survey the rest of my quarters.

There were floor length curtains running almost the full width of one wall, the window they shielded overlooking the sea, judging by the sounds of wind and tossing water. The wax magnolias that patterned my curtains had a background of the same columbine shade used in the bedcover and whoever had chosen the room's colouring had wanted the impression of grassland underfoot, for the deep pile of the carpet had the viridescence of early Spring.

A heady scent from the blossoms lured me from the bed and I walked barefoot to admire them. I loved the smell of the natural wood used in the long, built-in wardrobes and, I saw, the ceiling followed the design, being comprised of long, narrow strips of pale wood.

Tables, chairs, book shelves and cupboards were in the same light wood, some carved with floral and animal motifs; four lotus flowers, their stems wooden, but graceful, gripped a square glass table top that acted as a display stand for a host of dappled green figures.

I sat, crosslegged, before the figures. Were they antiques? An aged man with the features and dress of the East of ancient times, hands concealed in his full sleeves, returned

32

my stare coolly.

"Come here, little man," I said, and plucked him from among his emerald friends. He felt waxy in my hand, stiff and indifferent, yet with a definite charm that was more than visual.

"You look as though you've been carved from a mottled green Christmas candle," I told him, returning him to his space on the glass adjacent to three Chinese girls. They knelt, robes draping their bodies completely, one strumming a lute, another playing a strange, melon shaped set of bamboo pipes and the third clapping time to the music.

"You're enchanting," I said, and tried to imagine my hair smoothed back from my face, padded and rolled in sausages on the crest of my head, as theirs was.

I admired a green frog and other dark green creatures and then spotted the clock. Gone midnight and a suitcase balanced on a whicker chair still unopened, was obviously mine.

How many girls would pack their suitcase and look at it three days later not knowing what the contents were? Would I recognise the familiar items? I released the two locks together; the metallic sounds small explosions in the stillness. Then, reluctantly, I raised the lid.

There were lightweight dresses, suitable for the warmer Spring days and heavy bright sweaters and slacks for the days that leaned more towards Winter. Tunics, a kimono, underwear; flimsy nighties and a quilted housecoat in black and gold with trailing ribbons. Packed neatly round the base were shoes and a toilet bag with a drawstring and a hard-topped case with oddments of jewellery in. Nothing remained but a bumpy article swathed in a silken scarf. Prodding it gave me no idea of what it might be, so I carefully peeled back the soft layers and looked straight into the eyes of a raging dragon.

We glowered, while I examined him. Travelling at speed, front legs stretched forward, back legs almost flat, level with his tail, the yellow-green glazed body was supported by a scrolled cloud that tapered off in line with the legs and tail.

Had I intended him as a gift? For my Father perhaps? Or was the evil beast a well loved possession of my own. He didn't feel like mine but then, neither did the clothes.

"You'll have to go with the little green man for the time being," I told him and set him on the lotus table.

I finished putting away my clothes, then washed in the bathroom adjoining the bedroom. And I thought about the dragon and wondered how he'd lost a nail sized chip from his base, so that he wobbled, and whether my faulty memory was right in thinking he was a building decoration I'd once seen in a book.

Bed was more welcome the second time. I felt safe, snuggled down between the sheets, to relive the day; the farewells to Nurse Tulk and Doctor Byford. Meeting Father again; the journey past quaint old shops full of pixies on toadstools.

". . . cousin Ruth! . . ." The sneering tones of Dominic forced their way into my memory. Ruthlessly, I pushed him away to think instead of the granite and chalk cliffs of the coastal road until I'd had that first sight of the Dragon on the headland, waiting to pounce. I faltered a little in my thoughts, then cheered, recalling Nurse Tulk. I avoided thinking of the abrupt Doctor, dwelt a few moments on my meeting with Father, pushed aside, again, Dominic stepping from the shadows.

And, unfolding the evening past, Grandfather had welcomed us to Dragonseeds; Bella, Father's wife, had gone to sleep in front of my eyes; Neal had smiled a smile that warmed me and Hannah had warmed me too, with milk and honey. And there was Symon, my newly discovered half-brother with the closed face.

Still thinking of my kinsfolk, I fell asleep.

THREE

I had intended to wake early, take the bath I'd missed the night before and plan, as best I could, the attitude I should adopt to each of the people I had met in the Library. I recognised it as a form of defence mechanism and I was going to leave the whole arrangement open to change as, and when, circumstances changed. Instead, the swishing curtains brought me to sharply.

Hannah's "Good morning," told me who was letting in the daylight.

I scrambled up in bed, looking at my watch and saying, "Good morning, is it really eight!" before I noticed the tray on my bedside table.

My "Thank you", was spontaneous and brought a slight smile tugging at Hannah's mouth. No more than Dominic's twitch, but a smile nevertheless. That, and breakfast in bed started the day well. By the time the last crumb of toast had gone my spirits were soaring. The overdue bath, steamy and relaxing, built up my confidence even higher. Eventually towelled and glowing, dressed with care, I took a deep breath, bade farewell to my dragon, and left the shelter of my room.

How tired I'd been, emotionally and bodily, on the previous evening, I knew when I looked about me. It was as though I was seeing it all for the first time.

The landing I was on apparently formed part of a round tower. My bedroom was a segment of the lefthand side, facing from the head of the stairs, and immediately at the end of the landing light streamed through a vast window, floor to ceiling, on the round of the wall. Two more doors,

35

bedrooms I supposed, opened off the right hand side of the
oblong landing. The walls, washed in softest aquamarine,
were hung with long scrolls and pictures. The scroll nearest
to me, in mellow browns, pinks and yellows, showed mountains and pagodas, while in the foreground a peacock
strutted, all important, vivid, haughty.

"Do you like our peacock, cousin Ruth?" asked Dominic
softly.

As always, Dominic unnerved me. More so now, as I had
not heard him come behind me.

"It's beautiful," I answered truthfully, but inadequately,
I felt.

"And valuable."

He was watching me closely as he said it and for no
reason, I flushed. The hot unreasoning prickliness assailed
me, as always with this man; antagonism had been generated
between us within seconds and my confidence was oozing
away.

"Let me escort you round your new home, cousin Ruth."

I wanted a guide certainly, but I would have preferred
the easy-to-be-with Neal to show me the inside of the fortress. With him I could have enjoyed Dragonseeds and its
treasures, with Dominic I was over-aware of every action
of both his and mine. But, I said, "Thank you. You're very
kind," and in a fit of bravado added, "Cousin Dominic."

A flash of something like appreciation glowed in his eyes,
the only sign that he'd heard my sally.

Descending the stairs I kept my gaze firmly on the
dragons and willow trees, tightly entwined, in wrought
iron, and supporting the bannisters that lined the impressive
flight.

It was when we were passing through the hall that I
noticed the niche in the wall with the yellow-green dragon
—a twin to mine. Should I remark on it? I glanced sideways
at my silent companion and decided to risk normal conversation.

"The dragon . . ." I began, and at once was aware of his

more than ordinary interest in it. We might not like each other, but, ironically, we were very much on each other's wavelength and I felt his tension vibrating on my own nerves.

"Yes?"

"It's . . . unusual," I said weakly.

"Very."

"Is it rare?"

"Well, shall we say this was one of a pair and . . . something happened to the second one."

There was a hidden meaning to the words, I was sure, and he hadn't answered my question. I had intended to tell him of my dragon, but kept silent and asked: "What exactly is he?"

"A ridge tile. They're made for roof decoration in the East. Hence the half round piece at the base, where they fitted at the roof end, usually in pairs. If you're interested this original pair belonged to the Ming period, about 1368 to 1644 A.D."

"You mean it's valuable?" I was thinking of my dragon, sitting quietly with his green friends on the glass topped table. Could be he was a poor relation with his chipped base. I waited for Dominic's reply, trying to read his expression. It appeared to my over-anxious self that he was deliberately delaying his answer.

Into this uneasy silence fell Bella's contralto, "Good morning," and she was there, resplendent in a flowing kimono-type drapery, red again, with a large butterfly across her generous bosom.

"How are you this morning, Ruth?"

"Feeling much better," I admitted. "I had a marvellous sleep and Hannah brought me breakfast in bed." Resisting the inclination to ask how long she'd been up; it might have sounded rude and her eyes looked as though they were barely open, I said instead: "Dominic's showing me round."

"Don't miss the portraits. Dominic will explain them all to you, won't you, Dominic?"

37

There seemed an underlying meaning in the last few words, but her smiling cheshire-cat face revealed nothing and I thought I had probably imagined it. Watch it, I admonished myself, that's what was wrong with yesterday —imagined undercurrents. Today is different.

In the warm light of day the mosaic dragon underfoot was calm, almost benevolent, as my cousin led the way to the Library.

"This was Great Grandfather Adam's favourite room," Dominic said. "I expect you've noticed that this is one of the two towers that form the major part of Dragonseeds?"

I hadn't, but I nodded, and he continued: "This room is, literally, a granite shell, faced with wood and books."

I wouldn't have phrased it exactly like that, but I knew what he meant. The Library was lined almost entirely by neat formations of shelves, each shelf filled with leather bound volumes. Tall arches, divided by pillars, broke up the room into more intimate corners, and tables and chairs were clustered in odd groups. High above us, plasterboard had created a ceiling of splendid forests, bamboo and birds; elephants and snakes; from which the dragon light fittings thrust their way, leering down on us.

I admired a tiny willow tree growing from an enamelled container on a corner table, then we moved on and I found we had stopped facing a carved wall panel.

"D'you like it?"

I caught my breath. "Like is too mild a word," I enthused, forgetting for a moment the antagonism between us, entirely ruled by the delight the Panel inspired in me.

"Well, as your amnesia has probably wiped out the story of this carving, as told by your father, of course, I'll try and refresh your memory."

Bitter words sprang to my lips. With an effort I held them back. Now was not the time. But I stored up each jibe and taunt, each veiled dig at my lost memory.

"Yes, I've forgotten Father's version," I said sweetly, "Tell me yours." And I seated myself meekly on a footstool.

Dominic straddled a chair arm nearby, leg swinging. "Before I tell you the legend of the panel, of Dragonseeds, you should know more of Great Grandfather Adam's bride, Pink Pearl."

"Yes," I agreed.

"Grandfather was always a bit hazy about how he came by Pink Pearl."

"Tut, tut!" I interrupted, despite myself.

My cousin ignored me and continued: "As he made his money trading in the East, not always conventionally, he could have bought her. He didn't stick to the coast as many others traders did, but left a crew aboard the clipper and journeyed further inland."

"But wasn't that very dangerous? I understood that much of the East was closed to white people in Grandfather's time."

"So it was and it was extremely dangerous, but you must see that for that very reason Adam was highly successful. He brought back many carvings from ancient tombs and wonderful figures and jade and serpentine."

"And you think he acquired Pink Pearl on such a journey?"

"I'm sure of it. In the South West of China were tucked away numerous tribes that are still hardly known today. One tribe was totally unlike the surrounding peoples, having straight chestnut hair and fair skin. They were rich in herds and money accumulated by opium trading. Their other big money maker was slave trading."

"A very feasible explanation for Pink Pearl," I agreed. "Where would she originate from?"

"Possibly from Kweichow. Or she may have been one of the Minka, a race who built great temples in the past; now they give all their talents to wood carving."

"It doesn't matter where she came from, does it?" I said contentedly. "I'm quite happy to have descended from her. From what little I know of her she was a wonderful wife to Great Grandfather Adam."

He was eyeing me strangely. Not at all like the cousin Dominic I knew, mocking and sniping. Then his face changed and his usual expression settled on his features.

"I'm glad you approve of my . . . our common ancestor. Now let's return to the Panel. . . ."

"The legend . . ." I prompted.

So I sat and listened, spellbound, to Dominic's dark brown voice relating the love story of two dragons at the beginning of time.

They were, it seemed, royal offsprings from rival king-doms; both with the bodies of serpents, the faces of camels and the horns of deer. Their legs were tipped with five claws, the sign of Royalty in the East; while the wings of the female were fans of meshed gold to match her body, those of the male rose green and ebony from his dark, strong, body.

They met and loved and fled away together, followed by the curses of their dragon kin, and in particular the curse of the golden dragon's sire.

"What was it? The curse?" I said.

Dominic's smile was slow, enjoying my impatience. "It was that the progeny of the union should be endowed with all the contents of Pandora's box. . . ."

"So?"

"But in such proportions, good and evil, strength and weakness, that the mixture would cause the downfall of their descendants."

"You mean wipe out the dragon family?"

"Not all. The family line would continue, but the charac-ters of many of them would be so involved, mixed up, if you like, that there would be friction and destruction with them constantly. No, the old dragons didn't want a quick revenge, but one that would continue for ever."

"It's not a very happy legend, is it?" I said thoughtfully, stroking the dead dragons at the foot of the carving.

Dominic laughed. "Look at the top here. See!" And he pointed to where the two dragons lay close together, blissfully happy, unaware of the doom that was to overtake them.

"And these?" I ran my fingers over the oval, brown eggs, scattered between the many scenes on the Panel.

"Dragon seeds," explained my cousin.

Sympathy for the winged serpents was still with me when we walked on to see Pink Pearl, as set on canvas, in the Portrait Gallery.

The Gallery, according to Dominic, was the original connecting wall between the two towers—twenty feet thick in parts—tunnelled through. To me, entering for the first time, it was a splendid wide corridor, with a medallion patterned carpet running its full length, protecting the polished wood floor. There was the same plain wood ceiling as in my bedroom, with concealed lighting illuminating the portraits.

Bearded, Black Adam I felt I knew well, with his pirate's face and restless eyes. It was easy to imagine him on a clipper's deck, ever searching for new cargo to add to the spices and sandlewood, sharkskin and jewels that were his joy and his fortune. He was half turned in the portrait, as though seeking Pink Pearl, whose likeness hung, in a thin, gilded frame, next to his.

Out of a face shaped like a golden watermelon seed, the strange eyes returned her husband's regard with tranquillity and trust. The hair tightly drawn back from her temples and wound in a flat ended spool on the crown of her head, matched the black of her eyes. One slim hand held a pale blossom, but its beauty was lost in that of Black Adam's Bride.

Words could not describe this wife of Black Adam who had inspired the house of Dragonseeds.

"A woman in a million, eh, cousin Ruth?" His words anticipated mine and I could only echo: "A woman in a million!"

Reluctantly, I moved on to Justin Tregellas. Grandfather Justin painted some forty years ago, showing in his colouring the mingling of his parents' blood. But where Adam had radiated a brashness and love of living, Grandfather's character and feelings were hidden in the eyes inherited from his mother.

Grandfather's wife, Maria, ornately framed, as though to add interest to her sallow countenance, was next to him. Where Pink Pearl's hair had shone blue-black, Maria's was the colour of badly charred toast. Had the painter held some grudge against poor Maria, or, as I was inclined to think, had he done the best he could with his poor subject.

"Grandfather had no say in his choice of a bride," Dominic said, a laugh in his words. "His father chose Maria because she was from a good family, for her virtue and perhaps because of her dark colouring. Rather hard on poor Grandfather but it could be that she had a kindly disposition to make up for her lack of looks."

Eyeing the dour Maria, I doubted she had hidden charms of any sort.

The issue of Justin and Maria's union, the twins, Marcus and Fabian, faced each other from identical frames. Only the frames were identical, however, for Marcus resembled Black Adam and the artist had captured his crinkled eyes and half smile with heart tugging realism.

The brushwork suggested the same artist had executed my father's portrait, but the warm personality Marcus must have possessed, according to his likeness, was not shown in the second painting. Father's 'V' balanced above his nose was, apparently, present when he was a young man, together with the rather lowering expression caused by his thick eyebrows.

"What d'you make of our respective fathers in their youth?"

Dominic's question broke into my mental task of trying to analyse the twins feature by feature; to assess their personalities beneath the paint.

"I was older than Marcus!"

Father's footsteps had been lost in the soft carpet.

"Were you? How much older?" Then, as an afterthought, I said, 'Good morning, Father!'"

After his own 'good morning', Dominic seemed content to leave the conversation to Father and I.

"Ten minutes. I was born ten minutes before Marcus." The intenseness was out of place and I wondered if this small accident of nature was the only triumph Father could ever boast over his brother.

We moved on, a silent trio, to yet another dark bride, Jane, wife of Marcus. I remembered Father saying that she had drowned with her husband in the river where it coursed through the bottom fields.

Poor Jane! I moved on, pity fluttering in me; the vague sadness one experiences on reading of some tragic newspaper story.

So this was my mother! The sadness melted to be replaced by bewilderment as I stared at the painting, aware of my two companions studying me closely, waiting for my reactions.

They waited. I neither moved nor spoke. There were no words to be spoken, for, to my complete confusion the face meant nothing to me. She was just Joanna Tregellas, first wife of Fabian, with chocolate box, blonde prettiness and blue eyes.

"Blue eyes!" I said over my shoulder.

Whatever they'd expected from me, it hadn't been a comment on the colour of mother's eyes. I had the pleasure, at last, of seeing surprise shown by both men.

"Blue eyes!" I repeated.

"Yes," Dominic answered. "Very attractive with blonde colouring. Aunt Jo was a very pretty woman."

My cousin had been about five when mother ran away, Nurse Tulk had told me. A young boy would remember her short, softly waved hair, her outward appearance, but he would know nothing of the inner woman.

I spared a glance for Father. He must have flushed at something Dominic or I had said, for I could see where the pink was fading down his neck, and he was smoothing his hair nervously. Or was he just ill at ease as the three of us stood, cold bloodedly, inspecting his run-away wife.

"No memories coming back." It was a statement not a question from Dominic.

"Obviously not. Doctor Byford said not to rush the matter." There was anger in Father, I heard. "Ruth will remember in good time. I should be pleased if you wouldn't try to hurry things."

To forestall what could be an embarrassing discussion of me and my memory, or lack of it, I shuffled a further few feet along the Gallery and found myself beneath the insolent gaze of Dominic; a recent painting I judged.

"A good likeness!" I commented, without turning to meet the mocking glance of the original of the portrait.

"I'm glad you like it," he said, knowing well that was not what I had meant.

The last frame contained Bella, poised on the edge of sleep. I wasn't surprised to see her in a kimono of geranium silk.

"Symon will be the tenth portrait, when he's a little older," Father said.

"And Ruth, of course, Uncle."

Father was startled, I thought, then he smiled and nodded. "Yes, we must have Ruth set down in oils. I'll ring Evans this morning." He warmed to the notion. "He owes me a favour, so I wouldn't be surprised if he doesn't manage to get down here within a few days."

"Surely Ruth's not well enough to sit for any length of time," Dominic pointed out. "There's plenty of time. If you leave it a week or two the weather may have improved and she could, perhaps, be painted at the foot of the cliff." A single eyebrow rose a fraction. "We could call the painting Sea-witch."

The thought of Dominic actually considering my welfare, calling me a sea-witch, unnerved me. I turned eagerly to my Father to endorse the idea of waiting, but his hand was restless in his hair and I knew his mind was made up. Strange how quickly I'd come to know him; his quick notions, uneven temperament, interwoven with flashes of affection.

My thighs were heavy from dawdling through the Gallery and I was relieved when Hannah came to tell us she was putting biscuits and coffee in the garden. "And Doctor Byford's in the Library," she told Father, "waiting to have a word with you."

"Won't it be cold outside," I asked, knowing the pale sunshine had no real strength in it and was backed by a cold whining wind.

"Not to worry," Dominic assured me. "The Garden Conservatory is a continuation of this wall, partly built into it. It can be opened out in warmer weather. But you'll see. Come along."

The Gallery ended at an open archway, and we descended, via marble steps, into the Garden Conservatory. Left to myself on a bench, comfortably padded with russet cushions, I leaned back against the granite of the old wall and had a good look at these fresh surroundings.

Exotic flowers, in the greatest profusion, tickled my nose with their heavy pollen; their garish yellows and reds so vivid that I blinked in an effort to focus and make out more clearly the involved curves of the petals and stamens. Vines clambered up slender columns, their thick untidy loops—like some giant's knitting—crowding against the domed glass roof, causing hazy shadows where the sun trickled through the foliage.

From where I sat I could see the sliding glass windows that laid the Conservatory open to the outside garden in more clement weather. Eight or ten feet inside the window an ornamental pool was scooped out, continuing under the glass to become a part of the tumbling water that found its way in and out of the rock gardens, spilling down out of sight.

Bella sauntered in and perched her bulk on a block of

sandstone at the poolside. Immediately the still water became alive with slithering orange shapes that gulped down the fish-food she let dribble through her fingers.

"Hello again, Ruth," she smiled lazily.

A humming announced Grandfather Justin. His chair appeared, parting a bead curtain with much clicking and tapping. I'd not spotted the entrance earlier, hidden as it was behind a giant fern.

Neal was close behind the chair and I experienced a sense of ease to have him near; glad when he flopped on the far end of my bench, thrusting his legs in front of him and saying, "Hello."

Grandfather grunted a greeting. Did Hannah take him his breakfast in bed, I wondered; assist him when he left his bed? In his chair he was hardly incapacitated, twisting and turning with precision, but it was doubtful if he could manage to move himself appreciably outside the chair.

Bella played mother, pouring the coffee in leisurely fashion, each cup filled to a fraction beneath the level of a gold band inside the rim.

Watching my step-mother, I saw how her slumberous manner misled one; lack of speed didn't mean she didn't get through various tasks, merely that they were tackled in her own controlled way, slowly, thoroughly and with precision.

"Hannah's coffee is consistently good," Neal sniffed appreciatively, and I agreed wholeheartedly with him.

"And in lovely cups," I continued, meaning it but also wanting to encourage conversation.

"Dominic brought them back from his travels. They're paper maché."

"Goodness don't they go soggy in the washing up!"

A shared mental picture of soggy cups is a good basis for nonsensical conversation, I found. Stimulating to an ego that Doctor Byford had started to deflate and the sardonic Dominic had continued to prick.

Symon was near the pool and I disliked him even more

by daylight than I had the previous evening.

Neal followed where I was looking: "You might find your new half-brother a bit hard to get on with. He doesn't talk much. He's withdrawn. But I expect he'll accept you in time."

I bit back telling him that I didn't care if I never got on with Symon; that I was convinced he was a horrible, beast of a boy with his deadpan face and stealthy tread. Neal was Uncle to a little horror and as soon as I knew him—Neal— well enough, I should tell him so in detail. I'd tell him that . . . I paused . . . that his nephew was an illmannered, oafish boy.

Was he though? To be honest, was Symon so very terrible? Or was it me? Imagining an atmosphere that didn't exist, disliking the people I'd come amongst without justification.

Doctor Byford was here now, with Father. Would it be a good idea to discuss my overtaut nerves with him? Ask him if it was part and parcel of being an amnesia victim? The price would probably be a lecture on jay-walking, but I would risk it for a ruling on my up and down state of mind. Setting the bright cup in its saucer, I excused myself to Neal and made my way to the Library. Too late; only Hannah was there collecting a small tray and two empty cups.

"Doctor Byford gone?" I queried, half hoping to hear that Father and his visitor were still in the vicinity.

Hannah thought carefully for several seconds, head on one side like a pale grey bird, then said, "Your Father and the Doctor left the Library as soon as they'd finished their coffee."

It hardly seemed worth while re-joining the coffee drinkers in the Garden Conservatory. By now they would be abandoning their cups; my 'looking-round' tour with Dominic I felt inclined to pretend to forget. On considera- tion, my bedroom was a good place to laze away time before lunch.

Leaving the smell of old books, I slid my fingers over the carved dragons as I passed them, gave a quick glance behind the screen, half expecting to find sneaky-footed Symon, then walked, toe-to-heel—childlike—up the mosaic dragon's flames. I had intended to say a quick, 'hello dragon' to the ridge dragon in his niche, going by, and I'd actually said 'hello' before the fact that I might be seeing double struck me. For the dragon's lair held not one, but two beasts, and the interloper had a nail sized chip out of the base.

When you're taken by surprise, as I was, it's hard to say how long you stand doing absolutely nothing. It might have been three or four seconds, or minutes, that I spent gaping at the pair. It was a thudding sound that spun me round. Hannah's sheepskin slippers were soles towards me, her slight body a crumpled heap.

"Bella!" I yelled, dropping beside Hannah. "Bella!" again, more loudly this time, remembering the last occasion I'd seen her had been in the Conservatory. But suddenly she was by me.

"What happened?"

"I don't know. I was talking to the dragon in the wall, heard a sound, I didn't know what, and there was Hannah."

If Bella had looked surprised, I don't suppose it would have shown in the fleshy padding that submerged most of her expressions. Her lips did part as though to comment on me talking to the dragon, then Hannah gave a small moan and we both hung over her, anxiously waiting for colour to return to her cheeks.

"Joanna's dragon!" she muttered, gasped and opened her eyes.

"Stand back!" Bella commanded, picking Hannah up as if she were a bag of feathers. I looked to see who was to stand back and realised that the whole household was present; Neal and Dominic arriving as Bella carried her tiny burden, protesting weakly, to a chair in the Library.

Someone said: "Has Doctor Byford gone?" and someone else answered, "Yes!", while Hannah continued to tell us

48

that she was completely recovered and managed to stand on wobbly legs to prove it.

Dominic was close behind Hannah, the rest of us circled her, aimlessly staring, now that our patient no longer required our aid.

"Shall I take you to your room?" Dominic asked, but she was shaking her head before he'd finished. "What made you faint?" My cousin was persistent.

"Leave her alone!" Father's voice was unsteady. "You can see she's not well enough to be badgered with questions."

Dominic's face had a silky expression that I associated with trouble; Father's was a mixture of worry, stubbornness and aggression and he was smoothing and snatching his hair with desperate intentness.

The group was silent. I tried to think of possible words to use as red-herrings to wave in the faces of these two contenders in what promised to be a word battle of enormous magnitude. In the end, the cause of it all finished it.

"Stop it!" Hannah's voice was practically normal. "My potatoes will be overcooked. I'm going to the kitchen." And she went.

The anti-climax left us standing in a group, so we each found a chair and settled self-consciously in it.

Grandfather hummed up, using the arm of my chair as a brake, snapping my teeth together. Like Father, he looked shaken. "What did you say happened?" he asked.

I didn't make the obvious rejoinder, 'I didn't say!' Instead I told him, "I was looking at the dragons in the hall, the ridge tile dragons, and . . ."

"Dragons?" Several voices questioned.

"Yes! Someone has added my tile dragon to its friend in the niche in the hall," I said flippantly. "Come and see." And I led the way, Pied Piper like, trying not to think of my family as rats.

Looking again at the yellow-green beasts, I wriggled my toes, impatiently awaiting some comment. Having marched

49

from the Library ahead of the group, when I turned I faced them all. A battery of stares, concealing a miscellany of thoughts that I would dearly have loved to know. The hush too, was uncanny. Surely there should have been a word or two on my dragon's arrival in the niche, and more importantly, a small give away sign from the someone that had removed the beast from my room.

Bella had her knitting, I saw, and was idly puncturing the ball with the needles. Her son—I found it hard to think of Symon as my brother, even a half one—was by her side, his mouth slightly open, apathetic. And Neal? The likeness to his sister and nephew was unexpectedly there; utter blankness veiled his pleasant face.

Father's hand was gripping Grandfather's chair back and I knew I read correctly the two emotions uppermost in him; triumph, with just a hint of puzzlement. What could have brought these emotions into play within the space of seconds? Since Hannah had left to oversee her vegetables, in fact.

As I tried to sort out Father's triumphant something-or-other, I was aware that the atmosphere was exciting Grandfather. His wrinkles were puckered overtight, with bewilderment, then dawning surprise, then, was it pleasure? I couldn't be sure.

Lastly, I faced Dominic as he broke the silence. "Your dragon, did you say, Ruth?"

"Yes," I said. Then, unnecessarily, "Mine's the one with the chip out."

"I know," said Dominic. "I chipped that piece out years ago."

And his expression was the strangest of all.

FOUR

"Joanna took the chipped dragon. A suitcase of clothes and the dragon. Stupid!" Grandfather's face was gleeful. "Bet she was frightened to sell it." He caught my eye, remembered he was speaking of my mother and tried, unsuccessfully, to wipe the spite away.

We were back where we'd attended Hannah; sunk in the Library's low comfortable chairs, except that no one was completely comfortable. Family history was being resurrected—Mother's.

"Grandfather!" Dominic's tone was sharp and the point of focus shifted from me to my cousin.

I had not thought to get championship from that quarter, even one word, and searching the chiselled profile for a clue to his change of heart provided no answer.

"You might as well tell me," I said. "Is Mother the skeleton in the family cupboard?"

A small choking sound came from Father's direction and as I gave him a brief glance I saw he'd still not recovered from the worry of seeing Hannah in a faint. "No," he protested, "Joanna . . . your mother, wasn't that bad. It was just. . . ."

"She was!" Grandfather's shrill interruption transferred my attention to him. "She was a blonde hussy! No good! Carrying on with . . ."

"Grandfather!" This time Dominic's voice had the desired effect. The old man looked up into his Grandson's hard eyes and then clamped his lips together in two puckered blue lines.

The wheelchair was whirled with such savagery that it

51

squeaked, almost blotting out Grandfather's parting words: "As soon as you recover your memory, Ruth, you might remember what she was like. Though I don't suppose she told you the truth!"

Would I remember what she was like? Had I loved her? The portrait hadn't inspired any surge of tenderness. When an opportunity came I would return to the Gallery, by myself, and stand quietly willing the painted blue eyes to make me relive our past together. Hadn't I conjured up the misty figure of Grandfather Justin in his wheelchair, before I'd met him? I would try to think Mother back into my mind.

Close on Grandfather's sulky exit, Symon went, and Bella murmured that she would help Hannah and disappeared too. I wasn't surprised when Father and Neal went out, leaving Dominic and me alone.

"What you need, Ruth," he said, "is a cup of hot, strong coffee," and his fingers were firm under my elbow as he pushed me towards the Hall.

"I don't think we ought to bother them in the kitchen," I said half heartedly.

"We're not doing that. I'm going to give you a rare treat. Coffee in my room."

"Where?"

"In my bedroom!" There was a hint of the old mockery in the twist of his mouth, but the words were free of the bite that had accompanied much of his former conversation with me.

Unwilling to turn aside the olive branch being offered me, I felt a twinge of something, not fear, flutter in my chest. A speeding up of my breathing as though I'd run a race. I allowed myself to be guided up the stairway until we were standing outside the door opposite my own bedroom.

"You see, you're quite safe. A hop, skip and jump and you'll be in your own room."

I couldn't help the laugh escaping. "Did I look like a nineteenth century Miss? Shades of Maria in the Red Barn and the wicked Squire!"

"Are you suggesting seduction or murder, or both?" Dominic asked.

"Are you in the habit of committing either? On a defenceless cousin too," I countered, conscious that the door remained closed and my head was on a level with his shoulder. Drawing in a quick, shallow breath, I inhaled too the bitter-sweet tang of aftershave lotion.

A ship's siren rent the air and the moment was despatched; Dominic opened the door.

The coffee was hot and syrupy with brown sugar. I drank it, sunk in the corner of a settee by the window, overlooking the cliff drop to the sea. The same view that I promised myself I would paint from my own bedroom window, when I was more secure and settled. For the time being I was happy, very much at home in this room, its shape and fitted wardrobes replicas of my own, though the whole was in a reverse position to mine, tobacco brown, beiges and oranges were interwoven in the colour scheme and I saw here too there was a low, glass topped table, complete with green figures.

"You're admiring the little people," Dominic said.

"They're gorgeous!" There was a little ancient, a brother to mine. I stroked the tapering figure gently, wondering if he held some jewel concealed in his sleeve, to account for his secretive face. "D'you think he's hiding something?" I laughed. "Or perhaps he's just lost his memory!"

My cousin's face was quizzical. "It must be distressing for you, not recalling anything of your past life," he admitted. "What will you do if you don't like the memories when they come pouring back? Lose the lot again?"

It was a point that had occurred to me. Whether my past would be acceptable after being without it for a while. I touched the bruise that was spreading still, darkly blue, along my thigh, then fingered the ridge of stitches. Next week Doctor Byford would be snipping them out. Would remembrance come then?

Our conversation veered to the green figures and frogs.

53

"See this little creature?" Dominic said. "It's a cicada from an old Chinese Tomb. They believed that this larva placed on a dead person's tongue, eased the separation of the soul from the body. Interesting!"

I shivered a little. "And the other objects?"

"Some are genuine pieces—old—many our own copies in serpentine. The Ancient Chinese used serpentine, and jade, quartz and agate for their carvings. We're fortunate to have serpentine here on our land."

"I've never heard of it," I admitted. "At least, I don't think I have. Tell me more!"

"Well, the cliffs along this coast, near Dragonseeds, are fantastic. Mixtures of purple and red, with layers of green— the serpentine—in between. There's granite under Dragonseeds and, within walking distance, clay. Great white mountains of it, with milky green pools below, like Austria. I'll take you to see it one day."

My spirits soared at this mapping of my future. Possibly I had been a bit dazed, still shocked from the accident, when I had imagined hostility from the family. Why, at one period, I had really thought only Grandfather and Father wanted me. Their manner had not been overwhelming, of course, they were not demonstrative men; but they must have thought of me often and wanted me in the grey fortress of Dragonseeds, where they felt I belonged; why else should they search for me? Why?

Broodingly, I watched Dominic's brown capable hands set the cicada and the old man on the glass topped table; plug the coffee percolator in.

"Dominic!"

He spun round at the urgency of the word.

"Tell me about me," I begged him.

I was sick of the pickings of knowledge I had; fragments of Nurse Tulk's gossip, reluctant divulgence of information from Father; innuendos, or so they seemed to me, from the occupants of Dragonseeds. I wanted, I needed, facts, whether the Doctor and Father thought it was good for me or not.

I could have described what followed as a pregnant pause, accompanied by an indefinable expression on the face of the man scrutinising my own face.

Finally, he said; "What d'you want to know? Where shall I start?"

Where? Not knowing, I replied, "Tell me about Mother. The good . . . and the other," I said, as an afterthought, knowing there was bad.

"Right!" Dominic's voice was brisk. He drew forward a three legged stool and perched his bulk evenly, legs balanced and comfortable. "Your mother and father met when he was having a few days holiday further up the coast. From what I hear, Grandfather discouraged the twins from setting foot outside Dragonseeds normally. He always considered his home and the estate sufficient for himself and, therefore, as far as he was concerned, good enough for Marcus and Fabian."

"And your Father?"

"Was a charmer. Grandfather was not impervious to his smile and wheedling ways and I've no doubt that if he wanted to escape occasionally, then my Father did."

"And my Father, lacking that charm, didn't get out so often, I take it?"

Dominic nodded. "It could be that because he had to battle so hard to get free from his father, he lost his sense of proportion when he was away from home. Anyway, he met your mother and fell for her immediately. He managed, somehow, to court her and finally marry her, without his father discovering what was happening."

"Desperation drove him to find ways and means, I expect," I said, finding it hard to imagine Father forced to lie to Grandfather Tregellas; shielding his feelings and hopes from his twin. A thought struck me.

"You don't suppose your father knew and helped him, do you?"

But my cousin was shaking his head. "Happy go lucky my father may have been, but he'd never have conspired in a secret marriage that was . . . unsuitable."

I started to say 'unsuitable!' then changed my mind and listened.

"Eventually he had to bring his bride home, of course. Grandfather stated straight off that it was his opinion she was mouse, dyed blonde, and common with it."

"And you? What did you think?" I probed.

"The impressions of a five year old boy," he protested.

I was persistent. "What were they?"

The coffee bubbled softly in the quiet, then Dominic said, "To me Aunt Jo was like a princess from a picture book. I'd never seen anything like her pale hair; and the perfume she used. Very powerful it was." He sniffed and laughed. "Perhaps that's what Grandfather meant when he said she was common."

"That's not a proper answer," I told him. "What d'you think now, looking back?"

The coffee thundered in the glass dome, as he replied slowly, "Grandfather was right. He also insisted Aunt Jo had married your father for financial gain."

"And. . . ?" I prompted.

"And that was probably true as well."

Well, I'd asked for the good and the bad, so I couldn't complain. Beyond a quick tug of breath, drowned by the sounds of Dominic attending to the madly chattering coffee, I was careful to show no emotion, but steeled myself to hear a further instalment of the good and the bad.

Curls of steam rose from the blackness of Dominic's cup. I waited until he'd sipped half of it, faintly concerned that it would scald his mouth, but he said, "Lovely!" and raised his eyes to meet mine. "What else do you want to know?"

"Would you just go on talking, please. Tell me more of Mother and . . . me."

"Well your mother seemed happy enough. There must have been hostility, but at five I wouldn't notice it. She laughed with Father a good deal. I remember that. But he laughed with everyone. I don't recall it, but her moment of triumph must have come when she announced she was pregnant."

"That was me!"

"That's right. Aunt Jo went into Galston and saw Doctor Byford, to return with her news confirmed. It was about the time he was setting up his Nursing Home and, no doubt, you would have been born there if your Mother hadn't left."

"What could have caused her to leave at such an important time?" I asked. "Was there a big family row, d'you remember? Or had she met someone else?"

Dominic was faintly startled by my last question, I thought. Yet it hardly seemed likely that my mother could have formed an attachment with another man in so short a time. And opportunities to meet anyone else wouldn't be frequent. Why then has she gone without warning, leaving no message, taking hardly any clothes and only one of a pair of ancient ridge tile dragons?

"I don't believe anything but the usual bickering took place at that time. If there was a particularly earth shattering argument, I didn't hear of it. Another point too would be the little matter of money."

He didn't enlarge on it. I knew what he meant. Mother wouldn't go without a firm financial settlement; unless she was going to someone with money. She certainly would not have settled for one dragon, a chipped one at that. Why had she gone?

My thoughts concerning Mother's flight were shattered by a throbbing clang from the direction of the Hall. I jumped and Dominic said:

"One of Black Adam's little momentos from the East. It isn't so much the depth of the boom as the degree of vibration. Never fails to collect us for meals. So, shall we join the others for lunch!"

Hannah and Bella served the meal. Tomorrow, I would offer to help, but now I ate what was set before me and tried not to be overwhelmed by the Dining Room. It was the main room in the base of the second tower, I had discovered, taken through it by Dominic via more mosaic floors and alcoved doorways let into thick walls.

My wedge of melon lay in a pod-shaped dish, garnished with slivers of translucent glacé ginger. I ate it greedily, finishing first, so that I was at liberty to examine my surroundings.

One wall was as it must have been originally, its rough texture apparent, the windows hewn from the stonework reminiscent of the tall, peaked gothic architecture, once so popular. But could the builder of this old part of the Castle have returned to the present he would have been amazed at what had happened to these outlets on to the world outside. For some craftsman had chipped and fashioned, so cunningly, that now each window was transformed into a gilded Pagoda, the natural light that flooded in emphasising the strange beauty of the whole.

Were the tapestries real? Really old, I meant! Surely not! They gave the impression of having been woven centuries before, the over all colour faded, yet glowing a warm brown. But blinking hard and staring, I saw that there were varied shades in the ducks foraging in the reeds of the pool; the lotus plants.

The second course of the meal I spent working out what I thought half the items arrayed round the Dining Room were. The bronze mirrors I had read about, I was sure. One, over the fireplace, fascinated me with its grotesque beasts. No doubt the battles shown between tigers and dragons, wild boars and elephants, had some hidden meaning in mythology, but I much preferred the mirror depicting the signs of the zodiac.

I managed a little conversation and dragged my hypnotised gaze from an enormous sideboard against the wall opposite to me. It was so easy to imagine whole families spending their lives, carving and shaping its wooden body; the bulbous peonies and feathered chrysanthemums that made up the legs.

The cheesecake, speckled with sultanas, was so superb

that I left my study of the sideboard's weird beauty. "Marvellous cheesecake!" I managed, scraping up the last soft crumbs.

The tiniest of tugs at the corner of Bella's mouth told me who was the creator of this splendid last course.

"Marvellous!" I said again, "I can never make it properly."

Seven questioning stares were fixed on me. And I knew what they questioned. My lost memory. Initially, they had thought I was an impostor; not the daughter of Fabian Tregellas. The Dragon Ridge Tile that had disappeared with mother and returned with me, had proved my blood link with them. Now I knew what they were thinking—God knows why—that my loss of memory was all an act.

To be perfectly fair to them, my memory was such an inconsistent thing, erasing my past, yet throwing up titbits like the fact that I couldn't make cheesecake, that I could almost forgive them their doubts of me.

Father broke into the brittleness: "Bella's a good cook," he praised, "she'll give you the cheesecake recipe, or better still, show you how to make it."

"I can cook," I said, and knew I could. "If Hannah and Bella agree I can start helping, can't I?"

Father said, "Yes," and Hannah and Bella too, and there were little sounds of assent from each member at the table. With the exception of Symon, I was sure. I was seriously thinking of asking whether Symon did talk—ever.

So, soon after finishing coffee with Dominic, I was drinking it again with the others, after lunch, in the Garden Conservatory. Neal joined me on the bench and supplied the information that they alternated between coffee in the Conservatory and coffee in the Library. Where the tray was set down failed to interest me. I was more concerned with being again with the only person who seemed entirely friendly toward me.

"Like me to act as your guide this time, Ruth?" he asked agreeably. "There's a mass of this stone pile you've not been introduced to yet."

So I spent the afternoon with Neal.

It left in my memory a kaleidoscope of sandlewood chests, exquisite porcelain; paintings of willows and water, pomegranates and peaches.

On shelves and in corners were various ewers and fat-bellied vases and jars and red lacquer caskets; and in cup-boards, stored hard against one another, were snuff bottles and glassware with fluted sticks of glass winding on to them.

My mind reeled as we walked from room to room, up and down staircases guarded by dragons; by-passed the gun-room; admired the wild seascape from a dozen great win-dows, peered down dizzily from the battlements at pyramids of jagged rock awash with foaming water.

When a telephone trilled close at hand. I was glad to drop into a handy basket chair while Neal answered it. I propped my aching feet on the rungs of the chair opposite and hoped it would be a long conversation; but it wasn't.

"Someone asking for Doctor Byford," Neal explained. "From the Nursing Home. I told them he left before lunch."

"Probably calling on a patient or friends on the way back," I suggested.

"Well, it seems he hadn't intended to call on anyone else. At least, not according to the female on the phone. She gave me a graphic description of his lunch, a cooked one, congeal-ing on the plate."

"Nasty!" I grinned and we laughed in happy unison, pushing the wayward Doctor to the back of our minds.

I pleaded tired feet and a brain that couldn't possibly catalogue any more of Dragonseeds at one go, so Neal's guided tour was ended. We returned to our bench, to sit a while, casting our shadows over the fish in the pool, so that they came hopefully to the surface, making small begging plops at the water.

"Shall I feed them?" I asked Neal, noticing the food con-tainer partly hidden in the rocks at the pool's edge.

"Don't you dare!" I was commanded by Dominic from behind us. "They're fat enough as it is. Bella feeds them each evening."

He was standing near me, bringing the sweaty smell of horses, before I noticed he was dressed for riding. Neal had pointed out stabling and horses, toy like, when we had puffed up the hundreds of steps to the battlements to look down on the uneven lines and groups of trees that ran down the hill.

"Doctor Byford's got himself lost," I said to Dominic, vaguely wondering why he should be barefoot.

Intercepting my glance, he wriggled his toes. "Left my boots outside," he explained. "They're muddy. What did you say about the Doc?"

"He's left his lunch in a congealing condition, according to some irate woman at the Home," Neal said.

"Playing hookey, is he!" Dominic smiled and left us, to make himself smell sweeter, as he put it.

A bath appealed to me. I was grimy and tired from my tour with Neal. So I thanked him for his company and within minutes had reached my bedroom and shed my clothes. Bath oil and the radio from my bedside table; "Aaah! Dreamy!" I told the dolphin soap container, letting myself sink until the water reached my chin.

I should have tied up my hair. It floated like seaweed, tangling about my neck as I shifted position. I sat higher—Doctor Byford might not like stitches that had been immersed in bath water. But the music from the radio made me languid and, slowly, I slithered down again.

"Listen to the radio," I remonstrated with myself, "or you'll fall asleep."

I imagined the headlines: 'Long Lost Relative of Old Cornish Family Lost again in Scented Bath.' 'Relatives Inconsolable' would be the sub-heading. Huh! I doubted that last bit.

Thank goodness! A change of tempo! The Announcer advised a lively jig would take us up to news time. I splashed my foot to the beat until the pips sounded and a voice, drained of emotion, told of earthquakes, possible famine and political quarrels. I yawned, tried to concentrate on the local news that followed; fishing reports, records of sunshine and then, a boating tragedy.

How dreadful to think that while I'd been admiring the wild, grey sea from the tower top, someone had been fighting, unsuccessfully, to breath in that mass of water. ". . . body of a man was discovered in Merlin's Cove!" the voice continued.

Had I heard right? Damn my wandering thoughts! I sponged the wet hair from my ears and listened more carefully. He was speaking of our cliffs, below Dragonseeds. Well, the next Cove, at least. The body; could it be connected with the boating tragedy mentioned earlier in the news?

The pleasure of the bath was spoiled by what I'd just heard. I towelled dry, the sound of the water gurgling away somehow reminding me, uneasily, of the Cove incident.

As the soothing music resumed, I forced the victim of the sea, in Merlin's Cove, to the back of my mind. Instead I set myself to puzzling who could have stolen into my bedroom, removed my tile dragon, and stood him with his twin in the Hall niche. And had the person who had carried out the transfer understood the importance of the dragon being shown to the family? I was inclined to pick Symon as the culprit with merely spite as the motive.

Sea smells wafted through my open window. The curtains, pulled completely back, were caught on the edge of the breeze and struggled and billowed in useless puffs. I padded across to the window, enveloped in a towel, enjoying the coolness on my overheated body.

That view! It was a feast to the senses. In my mind I set out how to show it to best advantage on canvas. To the left of me the top of the cliffs were yellow with lichen, softening their sinister darkness. On the highest slopes the pinks and yellows of the wild flowers merged with the grass to form a carpet that my fingers itched to paint. And far

below, surges of foam pounded at the feet of the cliffs.

I leaned on the waist high rail and turned to the grandeur sprawled below, to the right hand side of the balcony. It was equally inspiring. The same mixture of colours, like confetti scattered on the stone and . . . and, "Darn it!" I wriggled my toes—they were cold on the balcony floor.

Stepping back into the room, for my sandals, without warning a new coldness touched the side of one foot.

'Spider!' squealed a cowardly voice inside me, though only a tiny squeak escaped me, as I jumped back. I allowed a few moments to elapse then returned warily to the window. Not a spider, of course. I laughed aloud in relief and bent down to the metal that was nearly invisible. Car keys on a ring. A ring decorated with a green stone. Not mine. At least I didn't think so. Whose then?

If Symon was the one who had pinched my dragon, then it was more than likely this was another of his tricks. A strange one. But then Symon was strange, not straightforward; he hadn't yet spoken to me. I wondered if his oddness was caused by an introvert nature striving to make itself known in the only way it could. Or did he just not like me? Resented me? The latter seemed most likely. In that case, the keys are staying in my pocket, I decided, and hoped that somewhere there wasn't some poor unfortunate being on his, or her, hands and knees looking for their car keys. I consoled myself by thinking of the unknown key owner searching out his spare key ring; no doubt also with a strange twist of green stone decorating it.

Dinner was strangely formal and I was glad that the long mirror had confirmed the rightness of my choice of a kimono in a delicate chartreuse shade, with feathery stitching in rainbow hues.

My hair had nearly been my undoing, had almost made me late for this first dinner at Dragonseeds. It was the fault of the trio of musical maidens on the glass topped table really. Those coils of hair! My own hair had been hanging plain and heavy on my shoulders. Suddenly, I had wanted to be like the green maidens. With the aid of a small flat sponge for padding and after several abortive attempts, I had achieved the polished outline that made my little musicians so outstanding.

"How about that then!" I smiled triumphantly at the trio, meanwhile dabbing my spicy perfume sparingly behind each ear. I descended to dinner as the last vibrations of the gong shivered in the air.

A small, colourless girl served dinner. Neal addressed her as Juliet, a name that hardly matched her rotund figure and sniff. Later, I learned that Juliet was also the maker of beds and sundry other daily jobs at Dragonseeds; scuttling mouse-like between her home at the far end of the bottom fields and her duties here on the hill.

Bella, sitting to Father's right and opposite me, had moderated her usual red to pink. A fluffy concoction like swathes of bloodshot meringue. I saw Neal look at his sister, wordless, then turn to me to smile approval of my appearance.

Grandfather was more outspoken. From the top of the table his thin voice travelled clearly: "God, Bella! Where on earth did you get that dress?"

Father, facing Grandfather, at the other end of the table, was torn between defending Bella and having an opposite opinion to his father. It was all there, struggling, twitching his mouth; indecision.

I was relieved when Dominic softly pacified: "I'm sure that dress is most becoming. Made for Bella, in fact."

We looked at him, doubting the truth of his words, and met an impassiveness that could not be pierced. Dominic the Peacemaker! A new facet of my cousin.

Because of the tension, I stiffened with apprehension at Neal's, "You look like a beautiful painting, Ruth," in my ear.

If Hannah was listening, it didn't deter her from eating her own meal and reducing Grandfather's food to small cubes for easier handling. Symon, facing Neal, chewed on, nothing showing in his face, neither pleasure at the food, nor ack-

64

nowledgement of any conversation round him. Dominic couldn't possibly have heard Neal's compliment. Or could he? He'd looked up at my mumbled, "Thank you," to Neal, and I had the feeling he might have heard the words.

Indigestion was settling like a rock in my chest. If I had my meals in my room would it help. As if in opposition to the one pain, my head started a steady throbbing. Changing my hairstyle had probably snatched my hair too tightly over my damaged head and caused the ache.

As soon as the meal was over, I would excuse myself and make for my room. The anticipated whipping out of hairpins to release my hair to my shoulders was the lure that kept me going until the last course.

We dawdled from the Dining Room, on the long walk to the main tower and the Library. A hand was under my elbow and I swung my head carefully to give a 'thank you' smile to Neal, but it was Dominic.

"Tired, little cousin?"

Was there the old mockery in 'little cousin'? Searching, I could see no trace of it, only genuine concern.

"My head is aching," I admitted, then with a burst of self pity, "And I've got indigestion."

"No doubt the origin of all your pain is Grandfather's unfortunate comments on Bella's ensemble." At least his true thoughts were shown. "You must learn to overlook these discussions. They'll be a good many of them. There always have been. Come, have you taken an aspirin?"

"No, but I have some here, in my bag somewhere." I dropped into a chair and balanced my bag on a table, foraging for the container; cursing the fact that I'd seen fit to cram so much into one small bag. My handkerchief dropped and Dominic retrieved it, sighing loudly, then laughing to prove he didn't mean it. But he didn't smile when he picked up the key ring, with the green stone, when it too fell.

"Yours?" he queried quietly.

"I . . . I found it . . . them."

"Where?"

I hesitated, then answered him, my voice equally low. "They were on my bedroom floor, by the window. They're not mine. I don't know whose they are. Do you?"

A babble of conversation was closing in on us. Grandfather's chair was humming nearby and Neal's voice said: "You're pale, Ruth. Are you feeling ill?"

I looked at Dominic, at the hand that held the keys. His fingers had closed over them, concealing them. "A slight headache," I answered Neal. "Nothing much." A lie, if ever there was one, for the ache had extended to my eyes and I'd hardly been able to see Dominic transfer the key ring to his pocket.

I gulped my aspirins as soon as Juliet passed me my cup, and prepared to suffer until the drug took effect. Father had heard I wasn't well and hovered, uneasy as men often are, when women are feeling fragile.

"Is it your head?" he enquired, over-anxious.

"Last few after affects of my jay-walking," I tried to laugh for him, but my mouth quivered. "Nothing to worry about, Father," I said, exasperation creeping into my tones, as I considered that I was trying to make him happy when I was the one in need of sympathy.

"Do you . . . do you think it's possible your memory is returning?"

It hadn't occurred to me that the pain might be tied up with returning memory. If it was so, it would be worth it. I was quite willing to exchange an extreme pain in the head for the return of my past—complete.

"Perhaps, Father," I said, and watched his face crease even more. "You must be the world's worst worrier," I scolded. "There's nothing to be done. Talk about something else."

Not much longer, surely, before the tablets blanketed the pain.

"I couldn't get Evans," Father said abruptly. "He's abroad. I've left a message with his wife and he'll contact me as soon as he returns. About a fortnight it will be. He's painting some tycoon. Pots of money, in America."

He went away and the conversation in the room broke into snippets of sound, sailing over my head. The tablets were working, soothing the pain, and my sight, which had been blurred, was clearing, so that I saw the nondescript Juliet when she ran into the Library, eyes bulging, intoxicated with her news.

"Yes!" yelped Grandfather, and would have added more, but Juliet was oblivious to any suggestion of reproach.

"The body . . ." she puffed, her small pasty face contorted with excitement. "The body at the bottom of the cliff is . . . was Doctor Byford!"

I looked across at my cousin, Dominic. He'd set his cup in its saucer with the tiniest of clicks, before raising cold eyes to mine. And for some reason I thought of the keys, and the twisted curl of green, icy against my foot, and I shuddered.

FIVE

We sat and discussed Doctor Byford, in hushed tones, as
befitted the newly dead; the family recalling small doctor-
patient relationships and me carefully not mentioning the
jay-walking in case it struck a wrong note.

Only Grandfather, the past as clear cut as yesterday to
him, managed to dig up an incident that jarred the conversation. "I remember the Doctor asking for a donation towards
his new Nursing Home. Just about the time you married
Joanna, Fabian." And the way he glared at poor Father
almost put the blame for the request on to him.

"What did you say to him?" he was waiting for me to
ask.

Grandfather forgot the Doctor was dead; his carefully pre-
served memory of the scene when the appeal for money
had been made, came alive: "Cheek!" exploded Grandfather happily. "I told him to go and earn his money."

What had the Doctor answered to that? We waited, but
Grandfather was smiling behind blank eyes, his brain enjoying the interview of twenty years back.

"You wouldn't think he'd never done a stroke of work
in his life, would you?" Dominic's irony was uppermost.
"Black Adam left managers to run the Estate, everything,
for him. He's my Grandfather and in my own way, I love
him, but he hasn't any values, in money or morals. He's a
selfish, egotistical old reprobate."

I threw a hasty look over my shoulder.

Dominic grinned. "Don't worry, I've told him to his face,
many a time."

"And what are your opinions on my Father?"

68

Dominic ignored the sarcasm I'd deliberately allowed to tinge the question. "Your Father? He loves Dragonseeds. He loves it more than anything or anyone under God's sky!"

A strange reply, but my cousin obviously thought it said everything. I tried another angle. "And does he work? Can he . . . is he allowed to do things for himself?"

"Oh yes. He and I do most of the managing between us. The fields that are sheltered, on the far side of the headland, and lower down, are given over to early daffodils, from January onwards. We tried mushrooms once, your Father's idea, but without success. Grandfather doesn't let him forget that failure."

The Doctor's donation request and Father's mushroom failure. Grandfather would go over them lovingly, often, I imagined. But Dominic was continuing.

". . . now, of course, we have the serpentine. Our true love. We're producing lovely pieces with material taken from the heart of Dragonseeds."

"And the carving? Who does it?"

"Local people. They have this built in feeling for the stone. I'm sure it's to do with them having lived on top of the serpentine for generations. But you'll see it all for yourself, eventually."

"And you? Are your activities restricted to overseeing or do you too carve the serpentine?" Could he read what was in my mind? I lowered my eyes, hiding the questions jostling there. Would Dominic's knowledge of the carved stone extend to his recognising a specific piece? Such as the curious twist of green—serpentine—attached to the ring of keys, for instance!

"Naturally I can carve it." Dominic pretended indignation. "You don't think I ask my employees to do work I can't do myself, do you!"

But I wasn't listening fully, for I knew, without doubt, that Dominic had recognised the key-ring. Did it belong to one of the family? If so, why should it be hidden?

Should I ask him outright why it was even now in his

69

pocket? I was staring at the pocket, unintentionally, and I saw that Dominic in turn was studying me.

Our eyes met; mine a wide-eyed questionmark, his an answering, 'be silent!'

Carrying on light conversation until bedtime was difficult, but I sat it out. Symon disappeared, without a word to anyone, so I didn't feel it was I who shackled his tongue. One day, I promised myself, I would corner brother Symon, and say 'boo!' or 'hello!' or some equally mundane expletive, and then I would only let him pass when I heard him speak; one word would suffice. Still, that was another day.

The present was ideal for sliding across to the sculptured Dragonseeds legend to study it in more detail.

The love softening the fearsome figures of the two monsters had been so perfectly captured; the large male's head was tilted arrogantly, hovering protectively above his smaller bride.

A little further down the Panel their troubles began; parental wrath—curses—portrayed by huge, glowering dragons. Onward into destiny; the dragon seeds, the fruit of the lovers, were scattered like brown nuts throughout the many scenes.

Halfway down the almond eyed dragonets broke from the seed shells, miniatures of their handsome parents, except for the expressions chiselled into each face; lust and a multitude of evils, but also love, compassion and goodness.

Could they possibly balance each other? They did in everyday life amongst mere mortals, so it was hardly likely that the same elements of character in the dragons would prove fatal. But that after all, was the curse! That the balance should be wrong, evil the dominant factor.

A tiny dragonet, appealing in his baby chubbiness attracted my attention. He struck a cord, some half forgotten scrap of mythology. The last escapee from Pandora's box! Hope! Yes, Definitely, the last dragonet, with his tiny claws still sheathed, radiated a simple optimism.

My attention drifted to the bodies of the parent dragons at the close of their lives. Their wings were folded in neat pleats against their armoured bodies, eyes closed, and a look of peace had smoothed away the worries connected with the curse.

Despite the confusion of the evening; the key-ring and the news of Doctor Byford's death, I clambered into bed happy.

I was convinced that the last dragonet to be hatched had been Hope.

On the second morning in my new home, I joined the family for breakfast, having quickly realised that mealtimes and coffee sessions were of major importance in the household, being the approved times for battles as well as orthodox eating times.

Having started down as the gong shivered into silence, I was surprised to hear Grandfather's highpitched tones reaching me well before I reached the Dining Room. Not breakfast in bed for him.

I said: "Good morning!" as I entered, adding, "all", as I saw that mine was the only vacant chair and the plates were already laden.

Neal pointed a helpful fork towards the sideboard. It was well protected by heat resistant mats against the mass of containers laid out. I lifted a lid at random and discovered heaped rashers of crisp bacon; another with kidneys; eggs and fried bread. The combined smells beneath my nose made my mouth water.

"How's your head, Ruth?" Neal called.

"And your memory?" Father tacked on the end, before I could answer.

"The first is better, thank you, the second hasn't improved," I reported.

I enjoyed the meal. I even enjoyed the backbiting and snarls of conversation. Already the sound of each voice, as it strained to overcome its neighbours and the din of the plates and cutlery, was a familiar background.

I ate, and talked, and partly listened to Bella telling

Symon to tidy his bedroom after breakfast, and behind that I heard Father, Dominic and Grandfather start on one of their endless differences of opinion.

"If it hadn't been for me insisting on a last advertisement in *The Times* you would never have found Ruth," Grandfather told his son, forcefully.

"We've tried so many times in the past, Father, you know that," my Father protested. "It's been a miracle finding her, so many years after . . . after . . ." he tailed off.

"After Joanna left you. Why don't you say it? The woman's been gone twenty odd years and still you fumble over her name!"

I was much too interested to be embarrassed. I studied Bella, my Father's second wife, across the table from me. Not a ripple of concern marred her face. Had she heard it many times before? Symon chewed solidly, entirely occupied in conveying food from plate to mouth. Neal was discomfitted, but only on my behalf, I suspected. Hannah crumbled her bread into uneatable pieces; Dominic, his plate empty, tapped a gentle tattoo on it with a fork.

And over the actors rose Grandfather's dialogue, in fragments, like Hannah's bread.

". . . still be married to Joanna . . . divorce . . . desertion . . . Bella . . . Ruth . . ." And then clearly, "I might alter my will again if . . ."

There was a stillness, a cessation of sound that was almost hurtful to the eardrums, as seven of us waited for Grandfather's final words. They never came. For Grandfather having created the vacuum, left it empty.

Bella pushed her chair back. "Come on, Ruth," she said. "I'll show you the gardens. If you're interested, you can take over the flower arranging."

So, protected by an enormous green hessian apron, with pockets, I sallied forth in Bella's wake; into the wonderland of gardens that was Dragonseeds.

What had previously been only views from windows, now tied up with the whole. The rockeries, draped in tiers

72

of pastel, divided by stiff mauve heathers, had regiments of tiny rock tulips; water ran in thin, shimmering rivulets, over shallow waterfalls from the pool that began in the Conservatory, down to where we stood, far below, continuing on its silvery way until it was a whisper of sound disappearing in the grassy slopes below us.

There were dwarf, pale green willows, bending their long, fringed arms over the water, making a cover for the birds as they sipped daintily and hunted for insects.

"Willows?" I queried.

"Grandfather Tregellas has the water pumped up for this garden. The stream and willows wouldn't be possible, otherwise. On the other side of the Pagoda, on the left there, you'll see more water."

So we dawdled on, down to the building with the turned-up roof, so that I could see the oval pond with its tile surround, spanned by a stiff wooden bridge. I feared for the delicate structure with the combined weights of Bella and me set on its middle. We leaned our elbows on the brown wood, rested our chins, and peered into the secretive depths.

Somewhere, beneath the surface, there was movement, causing the texture of the water to change and arrows of light to flash, blindingly, hypnotically, up at me. I flickered my eyelids, but didn't move, letting the heavy scent of the garden and the magic water take me over.

My head was crammed with black velvet, eyes full of crystal light. People walked on the black velvet, like an old film in slow motion. And, whatever was I doing in a telephone kiosk? And talking to Father too. There was a coach outside the kiosk and while I watched the driver got in and beckoned to me. Father was still talking . . . talking . . . and the driver was waiting . . .

"I've changed my mind!" I said loudly and slammed down the phone.

"Ruth! Ruth! Are you all right?" The very fact that Bella's voice was raised shocked me back to my surroundings, standing on the bridge.

The kiosk, the driver of the coach and Father's voice had melted back into the magic water.

"Yes . . . yes, Bella! I'm a bit muzzy, that's all. Don't fuss, please. It must have been the sun shining on the water. It's blinding, isn't it?"

She agreed and insisted we should abandon the flower picking.

Instead of struggling up the hill and into the Conservatory, Bella led me down the hill and round the end of a stone wall. By going the long way round we were faced with a more gentle rise to return to the house, through a lovely courtyard and out, via a strange circular doorway in the wall. Now, I was able to recognise where we were, in the kitchen that ran off the second tower.

"Really, Bella, we could have cut the flowers," I was still repeating, when we entered the Conservatory, to find the family gathered, and a man I didn't know.

"Ruth's not well," Bella was explaining, leading me to my favourite bench.

Grandfather's attitude was 'all this and you too!' but he deigned to explain the presence of the man, Edward Cargill, a friend of the family; a member of Galston Police.

Was it my experience at the fishpond that made my mind slip off at a tangent, so that the introduction of Edward Cargill was hazy? No, it was the faces of my family. I was constantly 'reading' them, I realised. And when I had them en masse, as now, I collected their reactions to a situation, a word, and turned them over and over, so that often I missed the happenings of the moments that followed. But my quizzical gaze had drawn stares in return, I found, and Hannah was suggesting a return to my bed.

"What actually happened?" Father was talking to Bella as though I wasn't there.

"A dizzy turn. She's not entirely well yet after that bang on her head." She lowered her bulk into a wicker chair, and

74

continued the conversation in my direction: "Whatever
were you talking about? Something to do with changing
your mind. You shouted it quite loudly."

Even Mr. Cargill was a part of the audience of interrogation awaiting an explanation. I hadn't one and told them so
rather shortly. For now that I was recovering, I resented
the morbid curiosity that was over-riding any sympathy
they may have felt.

"Social visit?" I asked Mr. Cargill sweetly, never doubting for a moment that it was.

He answered slowly. "Well, yes and no! It's to do with
the unfortunate death of Doctor Byford. I'm trying to trace
his movements up until the time he died. Only a formality,
of course." No one spoke, and he said, "We're still looking
for his car."

I watched a spider slide down an invisible web, from the
vines, and land on the knife edge of a fern that hung, like a
Damocles sword, above Dominic's head.

"Oh yes!" I said politely and unhelpfully to Mr. Cargill.
"He was here yesterday, for a while. But I didn't see him. I
wanted to ask him about my head."

The conversation lapsed and I could hear the fish blowing
air bubbles, on the far side of the Conservatory. After a
few minutes, during which conversation picked up, even
flourished, and Mr. Cargill learned nothing, he went, with
Grandfather humming behind him. There was an occasional
screech, as the spindle of one wheel sliced at a table or chair
and then silence.

Hannah and Bella said they were going to see about
lunch. I tried, in vain, to insist on adding my help to its
preparation, but was silenced.

"We're not giving cooking lessons to invalids today,"
Bella smiled gently. "We know today's menu by heart. A
favourite; duck in sour sweet sauce. D'you like it?"

I had to admit I didn't know.

"You'll soon find out then."

And I was left with the menfolk.

Dominic said, "I'll be down in the bottom fields if anyone wants me. Those last whites have to be packed today." And he too was gone.

"Whites?" I raised an eyebrow at Father.

"The daffodils. Narcissi, actually, in this case." He crossed to my bench and asked diffidently, "What happened in the garden?"

I made the story telling light, knowing how Father worked himself up. Neal's presence, perched on a chair arm would have the necessary cooling effect, I hoped. It did. He merely asked, as I ended: "What was it you changed your mind about?"

Grandfather returning, caught the last words. "What? What did you change your mind about?"

It was a bit of an anti-climax admitting I still didn't know.

A slight movement in the denseness of banked ferns reminded me that Symon was still with us. I couldn't see him, but imagined his ears cocked to gather in our words, as he collected most of the conversations in Dragonseeds.

"Fancy coming into Galston, Ruth?" Neal invited.

I thought of canvas, paints and brushes at once. The ingredients I needed to record the sunlight on the cliffs; the mysterious Pagoda pool. I ached for the stiffness of a brush between my fingers. And a palette, for squeezing out worms of shiny paint.

Neal could read my answer, but I did say, "Bella thinks I'm an invalid. Will she mind if I go out?"

"Bell mind? Nothing bothers my sister!"

So I changed into a lightweight bronze suit and tucked a scarf the colour of the April grass, in the neck.

Retracing the road to Galston was such a contrast to the journey I'd taken with Father. Neal, I knew had set out to please me and was succeeding. With this restful man I could appreciate a valley lined with gorse, that held a handful of cottages, set in cobbled streets.

We broke our journey at the halfway mark. A farmhouse, set on a rough track; all granite and lichened slate. The rhododendrons that had spread, untamed, framed the door-way in glowing splashes of magenta, giving a warm, wel-coming face to the place. And it offered morning coffee and cakes with cream.

A pixie of a woman took our order and directed us to a white wood table and chairs at the side of the building. I poured, enjoying the swirls the creamy milk made, as I passed Neal his cup.

Peace of mind was descending on me. The sun was un-expectedly hot and I lay back, eyes closed, absorbed in being a nature lover; a sun worshipper.

"The gnats will eat your cream cakes, dear Ruth. Eat them up like a good girl." His voice was teasing, warm on my ear.

Lazily, I narrowed my eyes. He was leaning over me, backed by a halo of sunshine that blurred the details of his face. Slowly, with deliberation, he touched his lips to mine. My lids drooped, shutting out his closeness as he leaned down again and pressed his mouth over mine; this time there was more urgency in the contact.

"Nice!" I said, "Very nice!" And when he moved closer, I laughed, and told him with mock severity, "I thought you wanted me to eat my cakes!"

We ate them. Not fully appreciating them, for both of us were engaged in the age old game of summing each other up. I, under my lashes; Neal openly.

Standing, I stretched and flicked away the crumbs trapped in my scarf.

Neal said, "Let's walk a bit."

But now I was anxious to reach Galston and the quick emotional togetherness I'd undergone minutes before, though still there, was something I was able to push into the background. Because he looked hurt, I took his hand in mine, and we returned to the car swinging our arms.

"I've an urge to return to the scene of the crime, so to speak, Neal. Could you drive by the bus station?" I asked when the road sign said Galston. When he didn't answer

77

immediately, I said, "D'you think it's a bit morbid?"

"No, no, of course not!" he assured me. "As long as it doesn't upset you."

"It could bring back my wretched memory."

"I don't think your Father would like it but, here goes. Bus Station first, Art Shop next."

We descended the narrow streets, twisting and turning, bounded by the usual granite buildings, their woodwork colourful and clean. Down past the Town Hall and shops with bay windows, into the bus station.

Nothing stirred in me; no panic welled up to flush out that which was hidden in my head.

"Would you like to sit here alone for a while?" Neal suggested. "There's a shop to the right there where you can buy your painting materials when you're ready. And I'll go and pick up those few things Hannah asked for."

When he was gone, I dropped into a seat and prepared to empty out any topic that strayed into the path of my subconscious. In theory, the minutest of details of my accident should now come flooding back and with them, I hoped, my elusive background.

I studied the buses and coaches, their passengers straggling across the main road where it touched on the side of the station. A silly place to shed a crowd of gossiping people. Much wiser to unload them in the bay where the vehicle eventually took on its new mass of humanity. I could understand how a stranger, such as I, with other things on my mind, had walked into the path of a car.

Re-living what must have taken place, made me aware of my bruises. The car could only have struck me a glancing blow, causing the blackness on my thighs. Possibly the cut on my head was the result of its coming into violent contact with the pavement at the end of the accident.

And what of the driver? Surely he knew he'd hit someone! Had blind panic made him—or her—drive on without checking the fate of the victim. Strangely, I held no animosity for the driver. How could I? Not knowing in detail the circumstances of the accident, except for Doctor Byford's opinion—my carelessness!

Theories! I wasn't going to remember a thing! I rose, fiercely resentful from my uncomfortable seat.

Turn to the right, Neal had instructed, for the Art Shop. There it was; full of charms and glassware, backed by Birthday Cards and Wish-you-were-here Cards. The door bell tinkled, I slipped between stacks of picture frames and found the department I wanted.

Tall, uneven sized brushes stood, bristles uppermost, in jars; palettes, some small and round, others large, like misshapen marrows, were there in piles, just begging to have squiggles of Raw Umber and Cobalt Blue, Burnt Sienna and Vermillion set on them. I hivered and hovered, telling myself I couldn't do without Cadmium Yellow and Rose Madder, White and Black and Ultramarine and Indian Red and Emerald Green. My heap on the shelf grew as I related the shades to the scenery at Dragonseeds.

A couple of sketching pads, linseed oil, turpentine, canvasses, charcoal, brushes; the assistant made a giant sized, brown paper parcel, firmly taped. I paid money from my wallet for the first time and staggered out to look for Neal.

I returned slowly along the pavement towards the bus station. Neal would look in the Art Shop, I guessed, and then the station. Nearing the unloading area I found myself enveloped by the passengers that spilled from the latest vehicle to arrive. They pushed and jostled as I fought against the tide of bodies, the unwieldly parcel slipping ever lower in my arms.

Perhaps it was clutching the parcel at an awkward angle and the unaccustomed touch of so many bodies that made me suddenly breathless. Or was it because I was being ricocheted gradually to the far end of the unloading space, where it met the main road, until I knew I must be standing exactly where I'd stood when the car hit me.

My head was wuzzy . . . feet leaden, and I could hear my own breathing, like paper rustling in my ears. There was a fearful sickness welling up with the terror as I prayed that history would not be repeated and leave me, petrified, at the mercy of the next car to swoop by.

The whole incident passed in a moment, yet it seemed an age before I was pushed out of harm's way, and free of the battering shopping baskets. Only yards away, near a wedge of open ground used as a car park, I spotted a telephone kiosk. It would provide a safe spot, for a minute or two, to stand the parcel down and recover my breath. Then I would find Neal.

The door was heavy. It dragged at my finger nails and tore a hole in the brown paper of my parcel. As I set it down, carefully, I was relieved to see the canvas showing was undamaged. I leaned my shoulders wearily against the shelf that held the telephone. I could feel sweat trapped between my scarf and skin, yet I was cold and clammy.

The little mirror at eye level was hardly enough for me to repair my face by, but after wiping my hands and face with a freshener pad and applying lipstick, I looked and felt better. I balanced the stopper from my perfume phial near the phone, while I dabbed at my neck with the fragrance. It was when I was replacing the stopper that I noticed the number in the centre of the dial . . . 27821. I recognised it instantly—the five figures I'd circled, darkly, on the hard back of my small notebook.

Why on earth should I have the number of a public phone box as the sole entry in my book?

I found Neal, later, and to his disappointment turned down his invitation to remain in town, sightseeing. The wrong sort of emotions were riding me for me to appreciate Cornish pasties, pixies and lobster pots. I wanted to tell him of the fear that had overwhelmed me prior to taking refuge in the phone box, then had a mental picture of the whole episode being discussed at dinner. I could have told him the story and added, 'don't tell anyone, please!', but even before the words were said, it sounded schoolgirlish and trivial, so I didn't bother.

To recompense for not being completely open with Neal, when he'd been so gallant and loving, I mentioned the 27821. I tried not to be upset that evening when he said, "Ruth had an odd experience today," and I became the hub of attention.

"Don't keep us in suspense," said a slitty-eyed Dominic.

Neal told them; embroidering the incident until it assumed an importance entirely out of keeping with what it was. At least, I thought so. Particularly when he finished off with a pretended fanfare of trumpets and then slowly intoned ...
2 ... 7 ... 8 ... 2 ... 1.

It was silly of me to make so much of a few figures pencilled in a notebook. They tossed the 27821 backwards and forwards like a bone, with a question mark above it until, finally, they were silent, staring at me.

The calculating looks filled me with unease and I shivered.

There were always undercurrents in Dragonseeds.

SIX

Very quickly I had slipped into the routine of my new life. No longer waiting for the gong to summon me to breakfast, for I was already helping with its preparation.

I had misjudged Bella's time of rising, I found, being fooled by that newly arisen look with which she'd greeted me on that first morning, when Dominic had talked of ridge tiles and Bella had sailed up, reminding me of a dozy red battleship.

My step-mother—though I always thought of her as Bella —was not what her outward appearance suggested. She had an active brain that controlled a body the unobservant might consider slow; but watch the two of us on the same task— potato peeling—and Bella's steady, unhurried fingers would strip the vegetables at twice my rate.

"I've been here a week today, Bella," I said, making neat cuts in bacon rashers and piling them alongside the mushrooms, for Hannah to grill nearer to eight o'clock.

"And?" said Bella.

"And it's beginning to feel like home, except . . . well, I would settle better if I knew more of my background. It's as though I was pushed into the world grown-up, a week back."

Bella smiled wryly. "Your Father should . . ." she began, then, "I think you're asking me to fill in a few of the facts as I know them. Am I right?" And at my nod she continued, "Well bear in mind that until now you were a very vague figure to me. To all of us," she amended. "Your mother had been gone several years when I met your Father." Bella's voice had adopted the tone of a storyteller, "And to cut a long story down to a reasonable length, we eventually agreed that a marriage between us had a very good chance." Not, 'we fell in love', I noted. "Grandfather Tregellas approved of a divorce for desertion being applied for, after a proper search had been made for Joanna and her child."

As the child in question, I felt oddly unreal, like a drawing in a fairytale book.

"No trace could be found of either of you and after a time the legal obstacles were overcome and we were married. Symon was born twelve months later."

"And Mother and I were forgotten," I said carefully.

Bella looked at me curiously. "I wouldn't say forgotten. You can't alter the past by pretending it didn't happen. Anyway," she laughed with genuine humour, "how can you possibly sweep the past under the mat with Grandfather determined not to let it be swept there."

"He talks about Mother?" A silly question, I knew, as I asked it.

"He talks about all of us, all the time."

It was true. Grandfather forced into his wheelchair, had converted his energy to mental and vocal use.

"But why should he want to find us? Wouldn't it have been better, when Father married you, and Symon was born, to leave things as they were? Is the Estate entailed? Does it go automatically to the next male in the line always?"

"Grandfather can leave the Estate where he pleases, but it's the Tregellas blood that matters, that rules who shall have Dragonseeds. You could have been a boy. No one knew whether Joanna's child was a boy or a girl."

"But Grandfather's sons, the twins, are the main line surely. Dominic now because his father is dead. And Father and. . . ." My father's wife was watching me with amusement, as I faltered, for it was obvious that any son or daughter of Joanna was Tregellas blood, through Father, and a possible heir as far as Grandfather was concerned. "And Father and Symon," I continued, though lamely.

I fished round for something to say about my half-brother's claim being the stronger, I thought, than mine, but the words stuck, and I knew they wouldn't have come out with a truthful ring.

"In any case, it isn't as straightforward as that," Bella had more to tell. "Grandfather plays a little game with us. One week he says Dominic is his only heir, the next your Father, or Symon, or all three. Finding you was not so much gathering in a lost Tregellas, as providing another pawn in Grandfather's game.

So I was a pawn! No wonder the tension had hit me as soon as I entered Dragonseeds.

I snipped the last rasher of bacon viciously. Hannah came in, glanced at the breakfast ingredients and set about the final stages. I said: "My turn to lay the table."

Dominic was standing by the sideboard and he gave me a fleeting smile as he bent to switch on the hotplates. He pulled open a drawer as I walked across to him, handing me the cutlery I needed, but with deliberation, one by one, delaying me.

"What is it you want, Cousin Dominic?" I asked at last.

"A little walk, a little talk! Cousin Ruth!"

"Now? Breakfast is coming in a few minutes. You don't want it cold and stiff on your plate, do you?"

It was a foolish remark to make, as I'd seen Dominic turn the hotplates on only minutes before. Also, I was reminded of Doctor Byford's dinner that had congealed on his plate while he was lying dead at the foot of the cliffs.

My train of thought caused me to ignore Dominic's question, instead I continued: "My stitches were due to be taken out tomorrow. D'you think I need to go to the Home. With Doctor Byford not . . . not. . . ."

". . . not. Dead!" He finished. "If you like I can take you down to the village. There's a Nurse comes in in the afternoons for a few hours. She'll soon whip them out."

"We could have our walk and talk then, couldn't we?"

Having settled my medical session, I dwelt pleasurably and with some curiosity on my intended outing with my

84

cousin. I didn't pretend to myself that I was surprised. I'd known the attraction was there, speeding up my pulse rate, as now, when he'd held a spoon for me to take, then let his fingers overstep the handle and touch mine.

There was a rattle of plates borne by silent footed Hannah, the spoon was released and I spent the next half hour surmising what might have been said, or happened, if we had not been interrupted. And hard on these fantasies flashed the memory of Neal's lips touching mine; with the scent of flowers and the sun's warmth in the background.

I abandoned my pleasant mental pictures and appealed to Hannah for some household duties. "Polishing," I suggested.

"You wouldn't notice last week, arriving late," Neal said from beside me, "but today's the day we are invaded."

I raised my brows.

"Cleaners!" came a chorus of explanation.

"We have a number of cleaners in once a week," Bella explained further. "Juliet flicks a feather duster over things for six days and Hannah and I work our way through the vases and mirrors and suchlike gradually."

"Well, shall I take over the mirrors for a start?" I suggested helpfully.

Bella was moving smoothly, collecting plates and cutlery in greasy towers. Even Grandfather pushed a dish half heartedly towards her. He does it to make believe he'd help if he could, I thought.

"Give yourself a little longer to recover fully, Ruth," Bella said as she passed me, balancing a last cup and saucer on the apex of her slippery pile.

"Well if you'll excuse me then, I'll set up a canvas and make a start this morning," I said, standing and pressing the chair away from me with my legs. It was as I straightened that I found I was looking directly into Symon's face.

He'd been about to speak to me. I read it there clearly. For an instant animation had shown in his colourless face, words had been there to be spoken, and then bitten back.

I was not mistaken. With my hand on the back of the chair, I paused, waiting for a word, a sign, but when none came, I left the room calling a last goodbye.

By the time I knelt before the low cupboard near my bed, smiling in anticipation of the brushes and fat tubes of colour, Symon was forgotten. I had arranged them in rows, grading the hues for my own enjoyment. Now I took them out in handfuls, together with brushes and a palette. And the oil and turpentine and a small canvas from the batch I'd left leaning against a cupboard.

There were fewer items than I recalled unpacking from the brown paper parcel and I saw I had forgotten one or two colours that I really needed. Stupid of me! But then, that day in Galston had been a very mixed one, ranging through the sweetness of the episode with Neal—cream cakes and kisses—as I thought of it, to the elation of my purchases from the Art Shop. Then, there had been my fear in the bus station and, finally, the uncanny discovery of the number 27821.

By the time I was organised for painting the earlier watery sun had disappeared and short flurries of rain dashed at my window. It was a disappointment, I had wanted to outline the scene by the Pagoda, where the water silvered into the enchanted pool. After some thought I decided on a different approach altogether; a view from the Garden Conservatory. A foreground of palms and ferns, the pool—divided by the sliding window—and the rockery that dipped away into the distance, leaving the Pagoda and its bridge as a tiny centre-piece.

I discovered a small cul-de-sac; a balcony of white stone, nearly smothered by the attentions of a mountainous vine. From this elevated hide-out I was just able to position my canvas and arrange my painting equipment along the balustrade.

Time flowed effortlessly, as I transferred my impressions of this unusual bird's eye view to the canvas.

A well known sound disturbed my concentration finally.

I tried to reject it, but it ate into my concentration and I laid my brush down with a sigh and peered over my balcony.

On the patterned flagstones below, Grandfather in his chair, reminded me of a spider sitting in its web. The stirrer-up of trouble! Often I watched, with fascination, as he contributed a word that would lead the conversation into channels that had never been intended. Harmony would be disrupted as the spiteful pebble caused widening circles of doubt to over-ride normal conversation.

If he could walk, would he be different? If? . . . I stared unbelievingly, for it was as though I'd willed him to walk. He wobbled and zigzagged, but he walked. What had lured him from his chair?

It was a whisky decanter! Cut glass, with matching glasses, set neatly in the centre of a wrought table, firmly hemmed in by chairs; unreachable by wheelchair.

He was clumsy pouring the liquid, but quick in drinking the generous measure, with an awkward twist of the head. I heard him gasp as the alcohol snatched at his breath, and then came a grunt of satisfaction. In no time he was back in the wheelchair, wrapping the rug over his legs with rough impatience, before humming calmly to the table where the coffee tray was usually placed.

I was left with one word revolving in my brain— hypocrite!

"A touching scene, eh, Ruth?" Whether I'd have heard Dominic if I hadn't been so engrossed in what went on below, I don't know. But I heard no sound until he was there, beside me, fiddling with the top of a tube of Red Madder and giving me a sphinx-like smile.

"You knew?" I answered his question with another.

"Of course!" His calm voice somehow irritated me and I was about to come back with a sharp comment when I became aware that the object of our conversation had disappeared.

Did the rest of the family and Hannah know Grandfather's secrets? I could ask my cousin, but when I turned to him I saw he was surveying my canvas through half closed eyes. His head was tilted back and his lashes made a wing of shadow along his cheekbones.

I forgot the many questions that littered my relationship with this man and acknowledged only the sensations that washed over me when he was near, a sort of pleasurable revulsion.

"Your fingers are covered in paint," I pointed out, to break the silence stretching between us.

Absently he rubbed his fingers together, spreading the colour, like blood, over his knuckles. A quiver started near the base of my spine and for some reason my thoughts turned to Doctor Byford and then blundered on to picture the keys that had disappeared as Dominic's fingers closed over them.

"You're shivering, Ruth. It's sitting too long on this draughty balcony." His critical eyes returned to my canvas. "But your time hasn't been wasted. I like the way the Pagoda ends the picture."

My quiver had vanished. It had been a quick physical happening allied to one or two odd mental pictures. Now I was overcome by what amounted to a head to toe blush.

"You like it? I'm glad! I shall add the pink rhododendrons here." I tapped with the end of my brush. "I was disappointed when it rained and I had to find a new position indoors. But now I'm sure it's the best thing that could have happened."

I screwed my eyes together, almost closing them, to try and take in the furthermost point beyond the end of the gardens. The more it rained the greener became the lawns that tapered into the fields below. Except for that one day in Galston, it had rained more than it had been sunny.

There was silence between us, but I left it and discovered that it was not uncomfortable, but companionable.

It really was amazing the amount of detail you could make out beyond the seemingly ordinary limits of vision, if you stared hard and concentrated. Where the fields ran away in the distance, there were trees set in groups, like bundles of matchsticks. Close to, they were probably very tall and old, I guessed. I allowed my lids to nearly shut and controlled my blinking, so that I was able to discover yet a further cluster of trees. A spot of colour lay at the base of them, against the dark trunks. There was very little shape to whatever it was and when my stiff eyelids were finally forced to flicker, my eyes refocused on a nearer patch of ground and the nameless thing I'd seen was gone.

Dominic was by me, wiping each finger free of the red stains. "What did you see?" he asked quietly, without raising his eyes.

"I don't know! What made you think I saw anything of interest?"

"Because in the short time I've known you, I can read you like a book. What did you see?"

"I don't know. It's just that in the distance, as far away as it's possible to see, in a group of trees, there seemed an unusual splash of colour."

"Gorse!"

"No, a stiffer shape. Why don't you look yourself!"

But his back was towards me. "Clean up and come down for coffee," he advised. "They'll all be here within minutes." And pushing aside the tangle of vine he was gone.

I tidied up my brushes and paint rags, screwed down the tops on the tubes and gave a final critical look at my painting. I leaned forward resting my arms on the coldness of the balustrade, noting small details that I would alter when I took up my brush again. And no sound, no sixth sense warned me when my second visitor slipped through the curtain of vines and thrust, with murderous viciousness, at the middle of my back, toppling me forward over the white stone shelf.

The flagstones were coming up at me, colours spinning. Shadows shot by like darts, as I fell. I tried to scream, but no sound came . . . I seemed to hang a terrifying moment, anticipating my own death . . . the impact. Instead the vine saved me, trapping one ankle in a great loop of green; breaking my fall with a jerk that drove the breath out of me.

A stupid picture came into my mind. Those victims of game hunters, stepping on concealed loops and hoisted in the air to await their fate. I knew how they felt, as I waited, my heart beating in my throat and the cruel roughness of the life-saving vine cutting my ankle.

I swung, one way, then the other, knowing I could still be dashed on the stones below. Gradually my body stilled. Blood pounded in my head and ached in the back of my nose. I was desperately afraid, yet I was regaining some control—thinking.

Whoever had pushed me would surely want to be certain they'd accomplished their work. Or would they prefer not to be seen near the Conservatory? But no, my death would be considered accidental. It was even possible my assailant was watching me now, only minutes away from coffee time.

Weakly, I cursed Dragonseeds and its constant coffee and meal times, seeming to come in endless succession, for I knew I would not be allowed to live until help arrived.

My heart stumbled. The grip on my ankle was slackening. I must make a rescue bid now. Risk swinging towards the centre vine and pray that I didn't spin.

Starting from my shoulders I swayed my body, very conscious of how much looser the grip of the vine on my ankle was becoming.

In the end, it was amazingly easy. I caught the strong main twist of vine, where it wound itself about a pillar, at the second grab. Then I merely climbed my body upwards, hand over hand, until I was upright and the stranglehold on my ankle relaxed. As I dropped to the floor, Father came in.

"My God, Ruth! Whatever have you been doing?"

I couldn't speak. Now I was safe, my legs wobbled and

the numerous scratches tingled. I felt as though every drop of blood had been in the wrong end of my body and was now rushing back to its proper place. A sound like a distant combine harvester echoed in my ears. And Father was staring at me, expecting an answer.

"My paints," I said faintly, combing my hair with my fingers.

"Paints?" His voice was incredulous.

"I dropped them off the balcony into the vine," I said and set about gathering the tubes that had fallen over the balcony with me.

Hannah brought the coffee and Juliet the biscuits. The family arrived instantly, drawn by the aromatic steam rising from the tall coffee pot. I looked at my watch. Ten minutes had elapsed since Dominic had told me to get cleaned up. I had lived and died a thousand times since then.

It was dead on eleven o'clock and someone in this room had wanted me dead by eleven, I thought ironically, and astonished myself by not being over-tense or frightened now.

What did one say? A murderer is amongst us! I could imagine the eyes; cool and patronising. 'After effects of her accident,' the looks would add and everyone would return to the more important pursuits, adding cream and sugar to taste, choosing an iced biscuit. I knew them well.

I said nothing and no one remarked on my bedraggled state or appeared to notice the raw graze on my ankle. Perhaps, added to the fact that I was daubed with paint, they thought my appearance was part of being a painter.

So I gulped the hot coffee then made my way outside into the drizzle misting the garden. Water soaked my open sandals, squelched between my toes, as I walked the lawn where it ran with the stream that trickled in a tiny Niagara to the pool.

I tried to avoid the wet arms of the willows and the shrubs, as I descended into the meadowland, peppered with wild flowers.

I had walked, without seeing, only thinking, and I was near the first clump of trees that had been in my view from the white balustrade in the Garden Conservatory. There was a thin tracery of green over the branches and birds' nests were threaded higher up. Within days, if the rain continued, the green would blot out the major branches and the nests. I leaned against the trunk of the lone oak in the group, looking down the grassland to other huddles of trees.

It was then I saw the man. He was moving at speed. Leaping small hillocks as the ground became rougher and fell away more steeply.

I stumbled as I left the support of the oak, but it was from an agitation that extended to my feet, rather than the uneven ground, as I perceived the running man's goal. Edward Cargill, before the end of his visit, had mentioned the Doctor's missing car was primrose yellow; Dominic had told me it was gorse. At this distance it was a lemon coloured car, dulled by mud.

Now, I was running too. Slithering and sliding in mud pockets. I heard the first laboured sounds of the engine as I was speeding between tyre tracks obviously made, at some time, by the car below. I wondered, had the Doctor driven it to this unlikely spot?

As I drew nearer I saw the extreme angle of the front wheels, the clumsy tilt of the yellow body and, also, I recognised the man.

"Dominic!" My shrillness rose above the engine, as it burst into life, and my cousin looked up, startled.

"Get in!" The command was harsh.

I ran to the passenger seat. Quite still while he reversed, I listened to the whine of the engine as the wheels churned muddy holes and spewed up brown spray behind us. Then my head jerked and we were moving forward, downhill. I braced my feet and gripped the seat, sparing only the swiftest look at the hard profile of the man at the wheel.

The windscreen wipers were noisy dealing with the

heavier rain and there were thuds beneath the car, but it was a small irritating, clicking that drew my attention. On the dashboard the curl of green serpentine, attached to the key ring, jostled and bobbed as the car moved uneasily under us in the mud.

Then we moved on to firmer roadway.

"Where are we going?" There was a quaver in my voice, though I tried to suppress it, while my main attention remained on the keys that I'd last seen in Dominic's hand.

"You wouldn't know if I told you. Just wait and see."

I waited, then said, "It's Doctor Byford's car, isn't it? The one the police are looking for!"

His, "Yes," was short and didn't invite further questions, but having started I wanted to go on.

"Why should the car be on our land? And in such a position?" A further thought came to me. "You saw it at the same time as I did. When I was painting on the balcony. You said it was gorse." He had also changed the subject, telling me to hurry and get cleaned up, I remembered. And seconds afterwards I'd cheated death and my would-be-murderer by becoming tangled in a vine, instead of crashing to the spiderweb of stonework below.

I couldn't believe that Dominic wanted or needed me dead. His hands on the wheel were firm, in complete control —like the man. Would those hands undertake murder? Mine? I had almost forgotten my urgent questions regarding the late Doctor Byford's car, now Dominic's answers came in carefully chosen phrases.

"Why should his car be on our land? I don't know! Perhaps he lost control and it ran down the hill to where you saw it. There's a dent in the nearside front bumper."

"But wouldn't he come back up to the house, for help, if that had happened?"

"Not necessarily! He might have decided the hill was steep and muddy and it was more practical to use this road we are on now, and get a bus."

I wasn't convinced. "If the car had run out of control

93

from the front of Dragonseeds, surely it would have followed the outside wall and finished up further across the fields."

"Perhaps!" His tone was non-committal and I had the feeling that the whole conversation, as far as he was concerned, was intended to convey nothing.

I searched feverishly for a further point of view to argue. None came, until the green serpentine clicked a sharp tattoo as Dominic braked, then stopped the car.

"The keys—the key-ring!" I said triumphantly.

"What about them?" His eyes narrowed and I wished, suddenly, that I'd left the unsatisfactory discussion alone.

"They were in my room," I said, braving the hard look and continuing. "The Doctor couldn't have driven off in his car if the ignition key was on my bedroom floor, could he?"

For a moment I thought I'd won.

"Surely you've heard of spare keys, little cousin."

At times when he called me 'little cousin' it had the sound of an endearment, now it had a metallic ring.

"Get out!"

I got out, to be met by rain laden wind that deprived me of breath.

Hunching my shoulders was instinctive, but it didn't stop me shivering as my clothes clung to me.

"Stay there!" Dominic lowered the window to call. "Don't move, whatever happens. D'you understand?" Numbly, I nodded, and he added, "I'll come back for you in a few minutes."

The wind was clawing at me, bringing with it the sound of the sea; angry water breaking at the foot of cliffs nearby, blanketing the engine's whine as Dominic left. Yet I knew I was standing in a slight natural dip in the cliff top, where pine needles had formed a wet carpet. I moved a few yards, seeking shelter and comfort from a gnarled tree. It acted as a windbreak but was useless as an umbrella, merely deflecting the rain, breaking its force. I was just as wet as if I'd been standing away from its spiked branches. But

Dominic would see me here when he returned.

I strained for the sound of the engine, tried to see through the mesh of sea mist that mingled with the torrents from above. Soon, I should hear the high pitched note of the engine complaining at being kept to a snail's pace. Soon! . . . but until then the scream of the wind, like a chorus of enraged seagulls, rose higher.

It was in a momentary lull, a freak silence sandwiched between the ragings of sea and storm, that I heard a noise I'd never heard before, but I knew what it was, without doubt. Without a single doubt.

It was Doctor Byford's car going over the cliff.

SEVEN

I crouched against the dank smelling tree, fighting to regain control and face the possibility that Dominic was in the car. 'Stay there!' he had commanded me and the force of his words held me still.

But my thoughts blundered on, conjuring up in horrific detail what the rocks must have done to the yellow car.

I heard myself whimper; my arms were tight bands across my chest, nails biting through the wet sleeves of my dress in grooves of pain as I rocked forward and backward, trying to push from me a picture of Dominic impaled on the rock teeth.

Stunned, lost in a grief that took me unawares, the noise of the growing storm mocked me with phantom echoes of the crash. And because I had completely given way to despair, I didn't hear Dominic return.

"Ruth!" The wind snatched at my name, carrying it from me.

He dropped on his knees and our two cold bodies merged together, combining wet and mud and a hungry rapture. 'Oh God!' I begged silently, 'don't ever part us again.'

I regained my feet, with Dominic's help and we stumbled from this nightmare field, until we met again the road that would take us back to Dragonseeds.

I hardly remembered the journey; dragging one foot after the other, Dominic carrying me the last few yards to the Pagoda.

"What happened?" I managed, at last. "Why did the car go over the cliff?"

Where our bodies touched, the misery of my wet clothes

96

was relieved, as we warmed each other, but I shuddered, waiting for an answer.

"It had to go. I ran it over deliberately."

I said nothing.

"Doctor Byford's body was discovered in the shallow water of Merlin's Cove. Right!"

"Yes!"

"The police searched the headland above the Cove for the car and didn't find it. Obviously, because it has been where you and I spotted it all the time."

"But didn't Edward Cargill check the gardens?"

"Only very roughly. A quick glance from various ground floor windows. After all he was making enquiries from friends, the Tregellas family, who assured him the Doctor had left."

"Are you suggesting that the Doctor left without his car?"

I wasn't sure what I was suggesting he was suggesting. But the necessity for smashing a car on the rocks of the Cove on the other side of Dragonseeds baffled me.

A man I had met briefly had perished and started a chain of events that knotted my stomach with apprehension. Part of me wanted to know what was happening, but the cowardly part was terrified and uncertain. Lack of knowledge was frightening, I decided. Not being able to ring my friends; not knowing who wanted me dead. Not understanding fully why Dominic should destroy the car or his true involvement in the Doctor's death.

But it was so easy not to reason when I was tucked in the crook of Dominic's body, his lips touching me, listening, not to his words but the timbre of his voice.

"Don't worry, Ruth! We'll discuss everything later. Now, we'll go to the house and if anyone comments just say we were caught in the rain. No mention of the car. Rest a while. You'll feel better!"

By the time I'd dried my hair and brushed the bits out of it, washed the freckles of mud from my legs and generally tidied myself, it was too late to close my eyes for the rest.

So I dressed and joined the family for lunch. Neal tried to catch my eye, but I looked to Bella and apologised for not laying the table. Her fork waved forgiveness.

"Have you had a good morning?" Father asked.

What could I answer to that? The painting was coming along nicely, but one of you tried to kill me and I am an accessory to destroying a vehicle being sought by the law.

Instead, I answered, "Oh, so-so! The painting is progressing, but I got caught in the rain later."

I felt Dominic criticising the bit about the rain, but I knew it was possible that we had been seen scrambling through the sludge of the meadowland.

"Couldn't you see it was going to rain heavily?" I did wish Grandfather wouldn't talk through his food.

"Oh, I don't know." Dominic enjoyed setting him off.

For once, I noticed a resemblance between Grandfather and Grandson. They both had the power to direct things their way with a few words.

"Didn't you see the clouds? Full of rain, they were."

"There was a little sunshine earlier on," I protested.

"Before seven!" Grandfather played his trump card. "You know what they say, 'sun before seven, rain by eleven!'"

"Grandfather is a great believer in the old sayings." Dominic was grave and it was hard to be sure if his tongue was in his cheek. "And the old legends," he added, "the tales of long ago."

There was a stillness, a suspension of activity, broken by Grandfather.

"The dragon-seeds story belongs to the East, not here. I've told you before. Because my father built Dragonseeds, doesn't mean the legend applies to us."

As no one else seemed likely to take up the conversation, I said nervously: "What exactly is the legend of the seeds?"

Dominic didn't say, 'I've told you once already' but: "The curse was actually supposed to be in the extremes of character of the dragon descendants. And it was these extremes that were supposed to cause friction, both in themselves and others, and the final downfall of the Dragon line."

"Absolute rubbish!" Grandfather scoffed, but we could all hear the underlying doubt in the thin, raised protest.

"Black Adam did lose his bride within a very short time," Neal pointed out.

"The damp climate. And he didn't build Dragonseeds and set up the Legend of the Panel until after Pink Pearl died." Bella entered the conversation.

"Besides," I interrupted the gloom, "the bottom of the Panel definitely shows a happy dragon. Maybe more than one." I vowed I would examine the dragons most meticulously directly after the plates were cleared away. "Anyway," I said, in what I hoped was a laughing tone, "What extremes of character have there been in this family then? And what misfortunes?"

In the hush, I had time to wish I'd not spoken.

Dominic rescued me. "Well, to start with, all the Tregellas are inclined to be well mixed characters. Apparently Great Grandfather Adam was a sharp tempered man, quick to land a blow at a crewman, though they all worshipped him. He was also a man of compassion and there are several tales that illustrate this trait."

I waited for the tales, but they didn't come, for Grandfather was bursting to get his next opinion to us.

"Maria died because of her own pigheadedness," he exploded.

"Father!" My own Father's cry came hard on the end of the blunt words that described his own mother; Grandmother Maria Tregellas.

"I'm going, Justin, she told me. And she went, riding that crazy new mare of hers, and was carried back on a gate." There was an I-told-you-so attitude to the whole recital of Grandmother's death, by Grandfather. I wondered if he had ever cared for the well-born wife Black Adam had chosen for him. If so, time had most successfully erased the memory.

The old man was in his stride now. Unhealthy colour made a triangle over his tight cheekbones, the opaque irises seemed clearer, lit from within by the strength of his malevolence.

"She wasn't actually a Tregellas, only by marriage," Bella said mildly.

"Doesn't make a bit of difference," he paused for effect. "Then there were Marcus and Jane." He glared across at Father, but no words came from his taut-faced son. "Damn-fool thing to do. Tried to cross the rope ferry when the river was in flood."

"Rope ferry?" I questioned.

"The roads were flooded and the two of them were due at a dance, or some such nonsense in the village. They tried to pull themselves across the river by the ferry rope and it snapped. Fabian was there, but nothing could be done to save them."

God! What a family I belonged to! The tragedies in their lives were trotted out, used as props in various arguments. And I had the feeling that they all did it. Changing sides and viewpoints; digging in the past for incidents to include in the recipies that made up their strange quarrels.

It's all happened before, this is a replay, I thought, and wondered if any of them was ever genuinely hurt by the words thrown in the exchanges.

Meanwhile, I was gradually being engulfed by their ways. The cheesecake, had been set before me, and I was tucking in as though Grandfather had not, a few minutes before, blamed the deaths of three of the family onto the short-comings of the unfortunate victims.

"Then there was Joanna!" The eyes above the triangle of brightness were on me, narrowed to cat-like slits.

I could tell that normally, when Grandfather started his cut and thrust tactics about Mother, he intended the wriggling to be done by Father. Now he had me. But I felt nothing; neither apprehension nor hurt. So I waited, standing outside myself and looking on, while Grandfather prepared to prod any raw places he thought might be showing. In the end I did a tiny prod instead: "What about Mother?"

"She was a Tregellas misfortune! She had no business in this family!" He might as well have said she was poor trash, for his tone contained it all. A hint of Neal's came to mind, that Mother had contrived her entrance into the family by the oldest trick in the world—supposedly being pregnant. The trickery and her blondeness must have guaranteed the hate of all the family.

I said, carefully, "Perhaps she would have been better married into an ordinary family. But I can't say, Grandfather, can I?" And as he opened his mouth, I added quickly, "Because I can't remember anything." As an afterthought, I said, "Don't forget Doctor Byford told me that in time I'd remember everything."

Father had Symon's habit, I noticed, of pushing a single item of food across his plate. When he saw me watching he laid the fork down and ruffled his hair nervously, facing Grandfather: "Ruth is not to worry. The Doctor told me so. When he visited . . . recently, he reminded me of this. If we argue about Joanna . . . her mother, we might do irreparable damage."

It jangled on, the bickering, becoming general and not quite so vitriolic by the time we reached the Conservatory. Helping with the washing up, I was not surprised to find the whole episode was completely pushed aside. Confirming what I thought, the quarrels were part and parcel of the Tregellas clan.

I said as much to Dominic in his den. "D'you suppose Grandfather causes trouble because he likes it? Or can't help it? Or because he's a secret drinker? Or what?"

He answered me over his shoulder, from across the room: "Have you given any thought to his upbringing?" He looked away, "I forgot your memory block. To make it short, his life was run for him; ruled is a better word, by Black Adam, until he was thirty and the old man ninety. His troublemaking is probably the result."

"But if you have suffered, been dominated in such a way, surely you would understand and not make the same mistake with your own sons?"

"You'd think so. Grandfather has tried to act the same as Black Adam, irrespective of whether his sons needed their lives directing or not."

"You mean that Black Adam knew his son—Grandfather —had to have discipline and gave it to him?"

"I'm certain of it," Dominic replied. "Then when Grandfather had his own sons, my father and yours, he ordered and interfered with their lives purely because that's how he thought it should be."

"And because he enjoys it," I said slowly. I sniffed. "What are you brewing?"

"Brewing is right." His laugh was light as he came towards me with a small lacquered tray. "Here, try this."

'This' was a steaming, clear liquid in a container that looked as though it had intended to be a champagne glass, but had found its slender stem squashed down to a short thick base. I sipped carefully, warned of its heat by the tendrils of steam tickling my nose. It was smoky flavoured, pleasant.

"Tea!" Dominic said. "You won't be used to the endless coffee drinking at Dragonseeds for a while, so, tea!"

"Nice!" I clicked my tongue appreciatively.

"And now the not so nice," Dominic said, so quietly I hardly heard him, only saw the beginnings of his inner thoughts drawing his dark brows together on the bridge of his nose.

His stool gave a protesting squeak as it took his weight. He set down his glass, then began: "The Doctor's body was left by the tide in Merlin's Cove. His car was on our land, the next Cove to Merlin's."

"But . . ." I said.

"Wait, Ruth. The morning before Edward Cargill came to enquire about the Doctor's movements, I'd been riding in the village. Mary Cambourne, the nurse who will be taking your stitches out, was in the main street. She told me the Doctor was dead."

"You mean you knew before Juliet told us? Why didn't you say when you came into the Conservatory? Is it because his death wasn't accidental? That you suspect something—someone—is connected with his death?"

I studied the impassive face opposite my own, willing him to supply me with facts that I could believe without effort; clear the riddles; the keys in my room; the Doctor's death, and the violent end of the yellow car.

"I don't honestly know why I didn't pass on the news immediately when I returned. Perhaps listening to Mary I sensed there was something very wrong."

"Suicide, you mean," I asked, almost hopefully. "Mr. Cargill didn't hint at it."

"Edward Cargill didn't say anything that mattered. But if he had had any suspicion of foul play he'd have searched the grounds more thoroughly for the car, I'm sure of that."

"What you're trying to say then is that you think there's been . . ." I hesitated, ". . . foul play. And you're basing it on nothing more than a premonition."

"And the car and the keys."

"What about the car?"

"I saw it when we were on the balcony. When you were painting."

"You said it was gorse!" I cried.

His eyebrows lifted, then levelled, before he continued: "I went to the top of the second tower with field glasses and confirmed that it was the Doctor's car; noted it's awkward angle. I was left with suspicion and one fact, that the Doctor's keys were found in your bedroom, near the window."

"And. . . ?"

"And I decided the car must go over the cliffs at Gull Cove. To add an authentic touch, I left the door open. It will be assumed, I hope, that the body was carried by the tide to Merlin's Cove; that is after the tyre marks of the accident are spotted at Gull Cove. Cargill will have already examined the cliff top at Merlin's Cove and found no evidence of the car going over there."

My tea was tepid and I sipped without enjoyment. Dominic took the glass from me. "I haven't finished!" I protested.

"I'll make you another drink soon, Ruth. Now listen to me. You're not a fool. You haven't asked obvious questions; because you're frightened of what the answers are going to be."

"I know! I am afraid! Dreadfully! I'm scared of the present and the past! You don't know what it's like, Dominic!" I was bitterly ashamed of the tears that poured down my face.

I was gathered up, effortlessly, and cradled against his chest. I wiped my fingers across my cheekbones vainly trying to stem the flow of wetness that was transferring to Dominic's sweater, but too late, the mustard was changing to damp patches of brown.

"Your sweater, Dominic. It's all w-wet!"

He laughed, rocking me gently. "Never mind. Let's get the rest of this business sorted out. At least as much as we know. Come on now! Buck up!"

Returned to the corner seat, I was looking down into the brown pools that were Dominic's eyes. With him kneeling there, my hands securely held in his, I felt brave enough to ask the question that hovered so long unsaid.

"Do you think the Doctor fell from my window? My bedroom balcony window?"

His, "Yes!" came back too quickly for me to immediately comprehend, leaving a second of blankness.

"I'd hoped it was Symon. Who left the keys in my room, I mean. I'm sure he moved my dragon. You know the tile dragon. And I'm positive he's had some of my paints."

There were other times too when the things in my cupboards and drawers had seemed, well, not entirely as I'd left them. Imagination? Perhaps! With a memory as full

104

of holes as mine, I was not inclined to rely overmuch on my faculties.

"Symon moves things," Dominic said. "But I can't see how or why he would get hold of the Doctor's keys and leave them in your room. No, it's not Symon this time."

"But what possible reason would the Doctor have for being in my bedroom? Do you think he committed suicide? Surely the landing window, between this room and my bedroom, would . . ." I was going to say handier, but it struck me as being a crude word, so I changed it to, "simpler."

"Suicide? No! As you said the landing balcony would have been a more obvious place. No, he was lured to your room on some pretext and pushed."

Murder! The figurines on their glass topped table became a solid sea of green. I shuddered and blinked and they became individuals again.

"Murder!" I said aloud, "Why? Who, Dominic? Not one of us!" It couldn't be Grandfather or Father, or Neal. It was laughable to consider the frail Hannah in the same breath as murder; or easy-going Bella. And Symon? He was only a child. "One of us?" I asked fearfully, knowing it wasn't going to be Juliet or the gardeners or a tramp.

"Who else but one of us?"

"And when I saw you first, going towards the Doctor's car. What had you in mind then?"

"Disposing of the evidence!"

"You're saying that if a Tregellas has done murder, you're willing to cover up for him or her, aren't you?"

He nodded quite calmly.

"D'you have any idea who it might be?" I heard the slight tremor in my question.

His shrug answered me. So the two of us sat, delving in our memories for any clue; a word or action that had some significance in the death fall of the Doctor.

"Come on, Ruth, I'll watch you make me a glass of tea." Dominic's hands were firm, as he assisted me to my feet.

I was glad to put aside the mental pictures growing in my head of one of the Tregellas hurling the Doctor from my bedroom balcony. I had hardly known him. Why had he had to die in the sea beneath my window? There was no sympathy, only resentment, for his untimely death.

I made the tea, following Dominic's instructions, and poured it into the lovely glasses. Our conversation veered back to the dead man. For an hour we discussed his death. We achieved nothing and, finally, Dominic rose to go; something to do with a new serpentine model. "Like the little Asian pedlar, with the flowerpot hat and high boots, in that group of figures in the Dining Room," he told me. I promised to admire the tiny man on my way to the Library, to look once again at the Panel.

I knew which group Dominic referred to. They were crowded together on a shelf, as though enjoying a whispered secret; inscrutable, wide sleeved men, acrobats and dancing girls. But where was the Pedlar man? I moved a honey coloured Buddha from the back of the shelf, but no figure had been obscured by the vast stomach.

Bella appeared in the arch of the doorway and I called across, "Have you seen the Pedlar man?"

"The Pedlar?" she repeated vaguely.

"Dominic said it was here."

"Oh yes! He's probably been put back on the wrong shelf, after his annual bath. Did you want him for any particular reason?"

"Apparently he's been brought up to date, recently. Copied in serpentine. Dominic says he's their latest model."

"Yes, that's it," Bella smiled. "He was measured and photographed, I remember. Funny little man he was . . . is."

"Never mind. I'll see the new streamlined model in serpentine," I told Bella. "I'm on my way to count the dragons to see how many happy ones there are."

The Library was empty. I dropped into the nearest chair, stretching my feet out, letting my body sink lower until it was balanced on my backbone. I was level with a clutch of dragon seeds and a shower of baby dragons had broken from their shells. I would have thought it impossible to show such varying degrees of feeling on the faces of the carved creatures; yet there was no mistaking the emotions.

Why there was even a dragon that worried its forelock, as Father did. And it had a 'V' between its brows too. "You really do look like Father," I told the beast, slipping from the chair and crawling forward to kneel before the Panel.

But now I was so close to the carving, I didn't care for the dragon that worried its forelock. It had a scheming look about it. "What an imagination you do have, Ruth Tregellas," I said, but couldn't stop matching the expressions in brown wood to the characters of the family.

The haughty one, high cheekboned, with hooded eyes; could it possibly be Dominic? It was a very ruthless beast, though handsome, like my cousin. And he was ruthless, particularly where the name of Tregellas was concerned. Hadn't he, with me as a weak accomplice, diverted the course of justice on this very day, with the destruction of the yellow car.

Somewhere among the dozens of sharp snouted dragons there must be a me, I thought. Not that obviously lustful creature, or the one that curled up, as though newly freed from its shell, sucking its tail, its eyes sleepy and devoid of intelligence.

Perhaps I was the one next to it, a small slim headed animal, with a bewildered look. Yes, I decided, that was me. At least, me as I was at the moment. Perhaps the bright, perky dragon was me when I had a whole memory at my disposal.

What a fool I was being. The Legend spread before me had nothing to do with the inmates of Dragonseeds. Yet unease persisted, overriding commonsense; flicking at my nerve ends, filling my nostrils with a mustiness that had no connection with the smell of old, leather bound books or the odour from the ancient stone behind the shelves and linings of the Library—the shell of the tower. It was more a thing of the mind; an impression of decay and death.

"Those damned dragons!"

I turned my back on them and within minutes the stupid obsessive ideas had faded out, but, unfortunately, too much reality replaced them.

How could I have so passively accepted the smashing of the car at Gull Cove? I asked the same question later of the three green maidens in my bedroom.

"You're tired now!" Their smiling faces seemed to echo my thoughts, adding: "You are irrevocably tied to Dominic now, for good or ill." And the 'ill' seemed most pronounced.

"But I was afraid!" I protested, silently.

"What of?" Asked the maidens, reading my mind, as I stood them in a row.

"Being found out, mainly," I admitted, without shame. Keeping to my inner self the tiny fear I had, of Dominic, and my omission to tell him of the attack against me, on the Garden Conservatory balcony.

That someone wanted me dead, I still had difficulty in accepting; like a bad day dream. Dominic could have nothing to do with it . . . could he? . . . And yet . . . and yet . . . Doctor Byford was dead and someone . . . who? . . . had wanted me smashed on the coloured flagstones. Unless— unlikely thought—there were two murderers under the roof of Dragonseeds, I must face up to the fact that the same person who had succeeded in thrusting a man from my bedroom balcony to his death, had failed with me and would try again.

EIGHT

My stitches had been snipped expertly out by Dominic's friendly nurse and on the way home I had told Dominic of the attempt to kill me.

In the re-telling, I realised how little information I had to pass on. I'd heard no one, only felt the savage hands in my back and then I'd been falling, the flagstones whirling up at me, until the bone-shattering jerk as my ankle had become enmeshed in the coarse fibres of the vine: like a fly in a web: but this time the web had saved the fly.

Dominic's, "My God!" could barely be heard above the metallic rasp of him messing up the car's gears. "Sorry!" he said shortly.

I watched his face tighten, the muscles tense along his jaw, before asking, "Well?"

"Have you any idea at all who it might've been?" And sensing the shake of my head. "Think! Shut your eyes. Now . . . was there no sound? Or even a smell that might be a pointer to who it was?"

I tried to relax and think back, but there had been no clue, I was sure, so I said: "Doctor Byford was pushed from a balcony!"

The remark seemed to stand apart from the rest of the conversation, until Dominic tied it up by saying, "And now the same person wants you dead!"

He was only putting into words what I had already thought, but it didn't make me feel better. I hunched my shoulders and to my own surprise, giggled: "Goose walked over my grave!" I said, and wished I could stop making stupid remarks.

I needed a Doctor, my nerves were jumpy. 'But look what happened to your last Doctor', a small answer came from inside me.

Dominic had ignored my shiver and was following his own train of thought: "At least we know Doctor Byford's death must be connected with you and, therefore, tied up with your arrival at Dragonseeds, as a new member of the family."

"You're saying it's one of the family, aren't you?"

"It has to be!" His voice was devoid of emotion.

"It's ludicrous, Dominic! Well, isn't it? Can you imagine Hannah creeping up behind me, in those sheepskin shoes of hers, and trying to pitch me over the balcony."

"Someone gave the Doctor his death push, Ruth. Keep that in mind . . . always."

"But . . . can you honestly think that Bella or Neal would do it? Grandfather isn't physically capable; Symon's a child."

"Children have committed murder."

"But we're the same blood. He's my half-brother."

His roar of laughter filled the car. "Ruth, Ruth! We're all related. It could be any of us. You haven't mentioned your father, for instance."

I hated that laughter. "I haven't mentioned you, come to that!"

He didn't laugh again, or say anything. We drove the rest of the way in silence because there were no words with which I felt I could dispel the uneasy atmosphere.

I stood in the shadows thrown by the pillars that led to the studded doors, until Dominic had driven the car out of sight, round the tower wall, towards the garages. A little further along the wall, in the other direction would be where Doctor Byford parked his car when he paid his last visit to us. Where had he gone and whom had he seen, spoken to, after Father? Dominic had said, 'You haven't mentioned your Father'. Could my Father take another man's life, if the reason was strong enough!

My feet were drifting as restlessly as my mind, and had taken me to the edge of the tarmac that circled the walls, to where it joined the grassy slopes and fell away. Away, to meet, eventually, that same clump of trees that had supplied a temporary resting place for the primrose coloured car.

"The Doctor must have parked it this side of the steps." Dominic came behind me. He rested his fingers lightly on my arm and I left them there. "It wouldn't be difficult for someone to release the handbrake. They may have sat in and tried to guide it, but I think not. The handbrake wasn't on and it was slightly damaged, so . . ." he shrugged.

"That would be after . . . after. . . ."

"After his death? Yes! The Doctor was presumably holding the keys in his hand and dropped them when he fell. He perhaps tried to save himself and the keys would shoot from his fingers."

Or were kicked away from my bedroom balcony, back into the room, by the murderer. The murderer! Another name for one of us. And it had happened in my room. It was not difficult to understand the keys being overlooked until their coldness had shocked me, touching my bare foot. The mottled serpentine would become invisible against my carpet's greenness.

Weak shadows zig-zagged down the walls as the sun tried vainly to find its way between the clouds.

"Dominic!" I paused, "About Father! He wouldn't try to kill me . . . would he?"

"And why not?" His laugh was mirthless. "If he thought he had a good reason, why not? Don't bother to say you are his daughter and blood is thicker than water. After a week in our midst don't you feel the tensions? Don't you see, we are, each one of us, a battleground of friction and unrest within ourselves! We are our own worst enemies! We love and hate each other with equal intensity!"

A shaft of black shadow sped across the wall, defying the sun. My heart felt as though it had been pierced through. "No!" I protested, loudly, to convince both of us. But I

knew he spoke the truth. The Tregellas were a race apart—
the Dragonseeds Panel come to life—and had probably been
so from their very beginnings.

"Cheer up, Ruth!"

How could he be so normal after what he'd said? I wanted
to lash out at him, at anyone.

"And Grandfather, and you, and Symon?" I mocked.
"We must consider you all."

"And Neal, and Bella, and Hannah," he answered as
quickly.

"They're not family. Not Tregellas blood."

"They are part of us! Contaminated by us!"

"I don't believe it! I don't believe any of it!"

But I half believed and the conversation was still twisting
in my mind when I accepted Neal's invitation to walk in the
grounds that evening.

I enjoyed strolling hand in hand with Neal. It was a
friendship apart from my devious relationship with Dominic,
marred only slightly by the fact that Neal had marriage in
mind. His intentions had been there, I think, as early as
when we exchanged our first kiss, sitting on the rough chairs
in the sunshine, on the road to Galston.

Tonight, as we sat in the little Pagoda, I needed Neal to
prove to me that life was not to be taken too seriously;
worked at, worried over. It was relaxing to my agitated
mental state to have his cheek against mine.

"How much do you like me, Ruth?" The words were
whispered.

"Quite a lot," I said.

"How much is quite a lot?" he persisted, his breath
making warm vapour on my hand.

Take care, I warned myself. Relaxation is one thing, but
there is a world of difference between liking and loving.
"Mmmm . . . well . . ." I hedged, wriggling my fingers until
they slipped free.

"Is it because we've known each other so short a time
that you won't commit yourself?"

Was that it? Did time matter to that extent? In the semi-darkness his searching look almost touched me, and he said suddenly, with a harshness I'd not heard in his voice before; "It's Dominic, isn't it? Dominic! You've known us both a week!"

My laugh sounded false, so I didn't risk words of denial, instead I said. "A week! It seems longer! . . . don't Neal, you're hurting me!"

I tried to prise his fingers from my arm; his hold became even more hurtful.

"It is Dominic, isn't it? Say so!"

This was relaxation? The mistakes one could make!

I slackened the arm still firmly trapped in Neal's grasp, hoping he would instinctively loosen his fingers a little, but to my dismay he caught my other arm and I was pulled closer to him.

"Let me go! You're being stupid!"

"Answer me then! Is it true? Is it Dominic?"

I gave up thrashing about. It was undignified. Dominic's words, 'They're part of us, contaminated by us!', came back to me. Was this the true Neal? Or had he been contaminated? And if I was wrong in my judgement of Neal, what of sleepy eyed Bella, and Hannah?

"What would you say if I admitted I cared for Dominic?"

The form of my answer; a question instead of a straightforward 'yes' or 'no' surprised him. I felt the tenseness slacken; his indecision came across to me and I used that moment to pull gently away, until the edge of the small corner seat touched my legs and I dropped onto it, releasing myself with my body's weight.

"Well?" I pushed the question at him, as temper replaced fear.

"I'd say the law of the land doesn't allow you to marry your brother!"

What I'd expected, I don't know. But it was certainly not this fairy tale. I burst out laughing. "You're mixed up, Neal," I said sarcastically, "the soft-footed Symon is my

113

brother, half-brother, if you like. You remember? Your nephew!"

"I mean it, Ruth! Dominic is your half-brother. Ask one of them! Hannah! Or your Grandfather!" The moon slipped from its net of cloud, showering the pool with light, reflecting shimmering patterns into the peaked ceiling, illuminating the triumph on Neal's face as he said, "Ask Dominic!"

I was held captive again. This time by the weakness in my legs, a sick trembling I tried to control by drawing my stomach hard in.

"Ask Dominic!" Neal repeated, and then, when I said nothing, "It's true, Ruth. I'm sorry in a way. I was jealous! Anyway you'd have heard it from one of the family at some time or other."

"You might as well tell me the rest."

He sat beside me and I saw, without surprise, that his usual pleasant expression once more cloaked his face. He didn't make the mistake of touching me or holding my hand, recognising the hostility I felt towards him. Finally, he said, "Why don't you just believe it's true and forget the details."

A flicker of hope must have shown in my face, because he went on quickly, "I'll tell you what I know. I can see you'll not be satisfied, otherwise."

An owl hooted in the silence, then Neal began: "Your father married your mother and brought her to live at Dragonseeds. There was a suggestion that she was pregnant at the time. . . ."

"A shotgun wedding!" I interrupted bitterly, thinking that I'd not heard one good word spoken of my mother. Well, one phrase; Dominic had said her blonde hair shone, but then he'd ruined the effect by mentioning that she used far too much perfume.

"Understand this story was passed on by the family in bits," Neal hastened to add. "Apparently, it was the old, old story, Joanna wasn't pregnant. Fabian Tregellas need never have married her."

I was once again experiencing the disembodiment, the sensation of being outside myself, as Neal spoke of my parents.

"You can imagine the marriage started off on the wrong foot, and it never improved from what I've been told. Joanna was never satified with the way of life at Dragonseeds. She hated it. The family resented her and she must have gone out of her way to annoy them. Only her brother-in-law, Marcus, laughed with her, teased her."

"But, surely. . . ."

"Oh listen, Ruth. Don't interrupt. I'm only passing on what was told to me. Later, when your mother did become pregnant there were doubts as to the father. I mean whether your father was really your father. The general opinion was that Marcus was responsible. Joanna knew what was being said and did nothing to repudiate it. So there you are, half-sister to Dominic."

"It's not very conclusive, is it? Gossip!"

"Those who lived with the whole affair seem to think differently."

Neal didn't attempt to stop me as I rose and left the Pagoda and I didn't look back as I returned to the house.

I met no one until I reached my bedroom. I hadn't intended to creep up on Symon, but my sandals made little sound and we were suddenly face to face outside my door.

"Symon," I started and put out my hand to him, "did you want me?" But my face, full of my own troubles, couldn't have been welcoming and he backed off, silent as usual, and disappeared down the stairs.

The ebb and wash of the sea, far below my window, was a sound I loved and found restful but, lying in bed now, torn apart by doubts, not knowing who to trust, to love, I felt fear pressing in on me with every thunderous crash. I let the night flow on without trying to sleep and as the first wispy light flushed out the night's gloom I was able to think clearly at last.

I must speak with Hannah. She would know the truth of

my parentage, surely. I tried too, as I lay listening to the gull's screeching, to be honest with my reasons for wanting to know who was my father. I'd become emotionally involved with a man who it seemed more than likely was my half-brother. And Fabian Tregellas? I'd lived the major part of my life without him as a Father, but I desperately needed Hannah to tell me that he was my Father now. "I'll be a wonderful daughter to you, I promise," I heard myself whispering, "if only you are my Father, not Marcus."

The clock fingers pointed to six thirty when I crept to Hannah's room. After my light tap there was no sound from behind the heavy door to show Hannah was awake, until the door opened for the width of her minute, questioning features. Topped by an elasticated cap, presumably disguising curlers, she seemed alien to the Hannah I knew.

"Ruth! Come in! No one's ill, are they?"

"No . . . no, Hannah. It's nothing like that! Nothing to worry about!" What a stupid thing to say, the bit about worrying, when I'd lain sleepless through the night worrying.

I sat down, at her invitation, apologising for coming; most of all for the time I'd chosen to visit.

"What has happened?" She was very small, sitting on the double bed, her wrinkled face uncertain.

"I don't know how to start really." My tongue was tripping, unsure where to begin. "It's about Father and his brother."

"Marcus? What about him?"

I wanted to shout, 'Is he my Father?', but it was too soon, so I said: "Would you tell me about him—both of them—the twins."

She didn't say that it was a strange hour to come asking for family history. Her dressing gown, quilted and smothered with clusters of drooping daisies, hung on the door. There was silence between us as she put it on and fastened a dozen or so pearl buttons, before returning to the bed.

"I loved them both, but Fabian needed me more than Marcus."

"In what way?"

Her eyes lost their focus as she searched her memory. "Well, even when they were babies, barely able to talk, Marcus had charm and was the one people remembered, liked to talk to."

"And Father?"

"Had rather a sulky nature. Underneath he was sensitive and passionately wanted to be liked. It made him do and say stupid things, being so unsure."

"Did they play together?" I said, instead of asking if the twins had been fond of each other.

"Oh yes! In the gardens, falling in the pond, climbing trees, exploring, breaking things. There was a strong bond between them, being twins, though they weren't identical you know!"

"They didn't quarrel then?" I waited and added, "Did they take each others toys?" And wished I'd had the courage to ask, 'Would one steal the other's wife?'.

Hannah's laugh rang out. "Quarrel? They did nothing else! Mostly because Marcus won when they raced or swam or . . . well, he won. And it was worse if Marcus let Fabian win. Fabian would know and nothing would pacify him. Stones flew, Marcus hid and Fabian was sorry later. They usually ended up, after the arguments, crosslegged in front of the Panel, talking to the dragons."

"And then Marcus married! Did my Fa . . . Did his brother mind?"

"Yes, I think so. They were still under the same roof, but naturally Marcus gave most of his attention to his wife, and it was another five years before Joanna Salkirk came into Fabian's life."

"Don't mind telling me, please, Hannah," I spoke carefully, "but how did the relationship between the twins and their wives develop?"

Sadness aged Hannah's face, as she dwelt on the past.

"Jane fitted in well enough. She was the only daughter of a gentleman farmer a few miles from here; a girl from these parts you see. Perhaps a shade too quiet for Marcus sometimes. He liked to be rushing here and there, talking and laughing. . . ."

". . . with his brother's wife?" I'd started towards my goal now.

The faraway look melted from Hannah's eyes as she appreciated the true question behind my words. Her mouth puckered. "What exactly do you mean, Ruth?"

"Hannah will you tell me . . . help me . . . please! You knew them all . . . you were there! Was Marcus . . . did Marcus ever do more than laugh and . . . and fool around with his sister-in-law?" I couldn't bring myself to say 'my mother' or even 'Joanna'.

I was sorry for Hannah, confidante of the Tregellas family, who loved them all, alive and dead. She had turned completely from me, while I pleaded, now she was facing me again. Ripples of thought passed over her skin, like smooth water undermined by raging currents. Finally, she spoke in a voice that was devoid of expression.

"You have never lived as a Tregellas, Ruth. Until your memory returns we do not know how much you know of us, what your mother may have told you of the family. Fabian found you again, restored you to your place in Dragonseeds. Does it really matter, after the whole of your lifetime has been spent away from us, whether Marcus or Fabian fathered you? The result is the same. You are here— a Tregellas!"

"But, Hannah. . . ."

It was too late. Her back was to me, unyielding, a shield over the past. And I was sure that Hannah was the only person who knew the truth. The others dealt in gossip, the end product of a chain of whispers since my mother had lived at and then left Dragonseeds.

I whispered, "Thank you!" and crept back to my bedroom, still not knowing whether I was linked to Dominic as a cousin or a brother.

I discovered a patch of warmth retained in the bed and slid into it, pulling the clothes high over my ears.

Dominic had said that he thought the Doctor's death was tied in with my return to Dragonseeds. Could that tie be connected with the question of which of the twins was my Father? Had the Doctor known the truth? I thought hard and long trying to see in what way the answer might affect the members of the family. Might affect one of them to such an extent that murder was the outcome; and attempted murder.

I was still jigsawing odd bits of knowledge; re-arranging it in my thoughts while I dressed. I had reached no conclusion on murder, amnesia or who I did or did not love, by the time I had snipped the bacon and was whisking the eggs in a fat jug ready for Hannah to scramble. She bade me 'good morning' as though I had never visited her bedroom, and as Juliet was early, and being helpful, I left the kitchen as the rashers started to splutter and made for the Dining Room.

Beyond a civil 'good morning!' to him, I ignored Neal's conversational offerings. Not because I was harbouring ill-will, but because I was too taken up with searching first Father's and then Dominic's face.

I saw two men whose eyes were dark, like mine, who bore a strong resemblance to me. But no clue as to the exact relationship that existed between us.

Breakfast over, Bella and I decided to spring-clean a few of the higher shelves in the Library. Poised on my toes on the top of the steps I surveyed the hundreds of volumes, greyed over by dust. The army of 'once a week' cleaners could never have set their steps at this level. Except for one scuffled handprint, as though someone had tried to balance themselves while reaching a book, the film was thick and even.

I flapped my cloth and showered clouds of the fishy smelling dust down on Bella. She was sneezing and laughing, waving a feather duster as the nose-tickling dust settled on the Dragonseed Panel.

"Ye Gods, Bella! Doesn't anyone ever read at this level?" I was spluttering.

"We couldn't even lift those books, let alone read them. As for cleaning, I reach as high as I can with this."

The gaudy bunch of feathers on its long stick was waved at me from way below. It was clear to see that it would never reach the top shelf.

I cleaned as much as I could while I was up the steps, vowing not to do it again for another ten years. I also leaned at a dangerous angle to blow the displaced dust off the dragons opposite me.

"Leave it, please, Ruth," Bella sneezed. "I'll finish the bottom of the Panel and then have a bath. You might as well get washed up now. You look like a ghost."

So I left Bella alternately blowing the dust, or teasing it from the carvings, with her feathers; left the grey film that had coated the books to admire, from my bedroom window, the soft mist that blanketed the sea. By the time I had stepped out of my dirty clothes and under the shower a shaft of sunlight was breaking through, casting a ray of light across the room.

Amazingly, when I had finished drying, my numerous problems seemed bearable. I took a little footstool and perched on the balcony, combing and sunning my hair to dryness; drowsy, contented. And because I was in a state between waking and sleeping, I didn't hear the door open.

The mouse-like squeak of the drawer I kept my paints in startled me. I stiffened, then turned silently, without rising from the stool.

Symon was kneeling, a tube of paint held close to his eyes, and I guessed that he was shortsighted. Slowly, he unscrewed its cap and touched a finger to the colour that oozed slightly from the nozzle. Yellow Ochre made a tiny peak on his finger, until it was squashed and smeared in the palm of his hand.

He examined the brushes and canvasses, and I knew that he had done this on many other occasions. At last he stood in front of the canvas showing the view from the marble balcony in the Garden Conservatory. The view I had been working on when someone had wanted me to die. I'd stayed away since, telling myself I would go back, sometime, even if it was only to prove I wasn't frightened. But I was scared and while I waited for my courage to return, I touched up the painting from memory.

Symon, I was convinced, had followed the painting's progress. Waiting until I was on the stairs, perhaps, before slipping from behind the wall cupboard on the landing, into my bedroom. Until today.

Now I had a clear view of Symon emerging from his chrysalis. The blankness was replaced by—could it be tenderness—as he was lost in his interest of the painting. I felt I was watching a naked soul.

"Symon!" I said softly and stepped into the room.

The curtain that closed out the tenderness, brought out the sharpness at the corner of his mouth, and the eyes became empty.

I almost asked, 'What are you doing here', but knew it would be dreadfully wrong. I changed it to another question as I picked up the canvas and held it to the pale light from the window. "D'you think I have made a mistake with the colouring of the trees near the bridge?" I said, and didn't look at him while I waited, hardly breathing.

It seemed endless minutes before he answered.

"N . . . no, I l . . . like it! The trees are b . . . beautiful!" The words were soft explosions. Not the stammering of someone who was nervous but the more difficult sounds of a regular stammerer.

"Oh good!" I said, still not looking at him. "I like another opinion and I'm a bit nervous of showing my paintings to anyone." I walked away from the window. "Can you paint or draw?"

There was hesitation again, then, "I t . . . try, b . . . but

I'm not very good."

"Would you like me to look at your drawings? Or are you shy like me?"

"I . . . I'd like you to l . . . look at them," a pause, then, "please!"

"Good!" I made my voice brisk, as I returned the canvas to its usual spot against the wall. "As soon as you're ready for me, let me know. Now you pop off while I finish my hair." And I left him standing there and shut myself in the bathroom. I heard the bedroom door open and close softly when he left.

I was humming a happy tune when I joined the rest of them for coffee. Even laughing to myself at the order of life at Dragonseeds. Each day was a pattern of meals and coffee; a meeting for bickering and laughing and settling business matters. A ritual that must be conformed to. But I didn't mind, I hummed. The encounter with Symon had produced a *joie de vivre*.

Grandfather's news, given after his second cup of coffee, added to the happy feeling. Edward Cargill had phoned with the news that the yellow car had been found and, as predicted by Dominic, it was assumed the Doctor and his car had gone over the cliff accidentally at Gull Cove and his body swept round the foot of our cliffs to Merlin's Cove, by the tide. The inquest would be a mere formality.

Dominic's devilish eyes said, 'I told you so!' over the rim of his cup and I couldn't resist an answering grin.

Two milestones passed in one morning; the death of the Doctor cleared and breaking the ice with Symon. My earliest trouble, the amnesia! Well, if necessary, I could live without my past. If, as the late Doctor had predicted, I should remember everything eventually . . . I mentally shrugged . . . so be it! I let my mind play around the most important thing in it—Dominic! I was convinced, in my newly confident mood, that the evidence for me being half-sister to Dominic was laughable. The tittle tattle of a tight knit family against a newcomer—my mother—years before.

Even the conversation with Hannah, on examination, had been coloured by a sleepless night, Neal's jealous outburst, and what could only be thought of later as incertitude on Hannah's part.

So my grin to Dominic developed into a full sized smile. At once he started towards me, his normally long stride cut down to side steps as he threaded past Grandfather's chair and the table where Symon sat with his mother.

"Cousin Ruth!" he said, very softly.

"Cousin Dominic!" I answered hardly above a whisper.

Grandfather was squinting across at us, so I said loudly for his benefit: "I couldn't find your Pedlar man, Dominic. D'you think he's been kidnapped?"

Father, from a few yards distance, said, "He was there yesterday, I'm positive," and Hannah and Bella both said, "He's been cleaned."

The wheelchair sounded like a chalk on a blackboard as Grandfather brought it round too quickly, pushing aside the tables with a great scraping of their bases, until he was opposite me. "The Pedlar. Don't tell me that's gone too?"

"It's about somewhere, Grandfather, I expect," Dominic soothed. "I'll find it. It may have been returned to the wrong shelf."

I thought of the paints missing from my room and the ornaments that changed places. Symon? The others were watching him too.

"Leave it to me," Dominic said again, and the old man nodded, only partly mollified.

"What exactly were the undercurrents there?" I asked, when there were just the two of us. "Was it to do with Symon and his . . ." I sought for a kind word, ". . . funny ways?"

"Funny ways! Mmmm! That's one way of putting it, I suppose. No it's not Symon. The figure has gone and it's as well to consider it's worth a good deal of money."

"Then who? And how can you be sure it isn't Symon?"

"Who?" He shrugged. "As for Symon. If he hides an

123

object, within days it turns up again, on another shelf, in a different cabinet. One gets used to Symon's funny ways."

"Then it may be discovered soon. When did you see it last, Dominic?"

He frowned. "Well, I went to look at it after I'd mentioned it to you and, naturally, it wasn't there. I checked dozens of shelves and cupboards—nothing! So it must be several weeks since I actually handled it."

"Father said it was there yesterday," I reminded Dominic and wondered, as I spoke, if Father was covering for Symon.

The thought of the costly little man, for the time being mislaid, was rather horrifying. But then I'd been shocked, ever since living at Dragonseeds, by the casual way priceless treasures were displayed, without protection from over-active dusters, or burglars.

"If Grandfather is so fond of the house and its contents, why doesn't he protect it? Buy a few enormous dogs!" I asked. "Or at least have a good alarm system against possible theft."

"You'd be in trouble selling, or rather trying to sell many of the items that clutter the place. They are too rare and would be spotted and queried before being bought. It's not like a haul of silverware. Now that would be profitable!"

"But . . ." I quibbled, a hundred and one arguments on the tip of my tongue.

"You can save your breath," Dominic grinned. "Grandfather doesn't hold with Insurance Companies either."

So I saved my breath but resolved to have a look for the lost mannikin.

NINE

I was anxious to follow up my first talk with Symon, but wary of scaring him off. In the end, I filled a carrier bag with paints and brushes and went to his bedroom. I knocked lightly, not intending to draw attention to my visit. No one did notice, but neither did Symon appear. On the spur of the moment I turned the knob and went in.

"Symon!" I called, "It's Ruth!" Still no reply.

I wandered across the room to glance along the bookshelf beside the bed. There was a well thumbed Nursery Rhyme book, a volume of poems; a tall thin book of castles in Cornwall. Next to the castles was a book on Pirates and then Treasure Island, Robin Hood and Robinson Crusoe.

It was the smell that drew me from the books and guided me to my lost paints. The carrier I had brought with me still lay on the floor by the door, so the oily aroma had to belong to resident paints. They were laid carefully on a newspaper in the front of a low cupboard drawer, but a cap had become loose on a tube and betrayed their whereabouts to me. Idly I removed the wobbly cap from the tube of white and touched my finger to the open top. When the door opened and Symon came in I was standing with an Everest of paint on my forefinger.

Disbelief, a touch of fear, then comprehension broke through the barriers of his usually unresponsive face. Finally, to my delight he laughed; "S . . . Snap!" he said.

Snap? I was slow to understand. Then I chuckled too, as I rubbed the soft whiteness away into my fingers, recalling as I walked to him now, the occasion I had discovered him in my bedroom with the tube of Yellow Ochre.

Silence greeted the canvas, extra paints, brushes and other items from the carrier bag. But it was a silence of speechless thanks and I understood.

How could I have been so blind? This boy I had taken at face value, failing to see his hopelessly inverted nature; walled behind impassiveness and a lack of words; living in the adventures of bygone heroes; entering everyday life on as few occasions as possible, swopping ornaments—a pin-prick of envy to try and pierce in a small way the confidence we appeared to have and he lacked.

"Let me see your paintings and drawings, Symon," I said.

"There's only one p . . . painting," he answered, but he was fetching it for me from its hiding place.

I had no pre-conceived idea of what Symon might try to portray on his small, stolen canvas, but my gasp was quite involuntary.

The scene, through his bedroom window, bore no resemblance to mine. His was misty enchantment, a kaleidoscope of flower shapes, tumbling water and fields, dappled by trees. I could smell the heavy perfume from this waterlogged landscape.

"It's beautiful!" I breathed and knew that here was a genius.

"I've got drawings t . . . too!"

There were hundreds of them. Many on brown paper and envelopes. Anything and everything had supplied Symon with models. My green maidens were here and a tile dragon —mine—its chip faithfully recorded.

"Did you take my dragon and put it with the second one in the hall?" I asked casually.

And just as casually he answered; "Yes!"

"And the Pedlar? Have you moved or taken the Pedlar?" "No!"

That was all. The rest of our conversation was of light and shade and colour; a new bond between us, sealed by a bag of painting bits and pieces.

"Goodness, Symon, we've been chattering for ages!" I

said, hardly able to appreciate that I'd conversed with this boy, not noticing his hesitant speech, for so long. "I'll have to go!"

I didn't mention to Symon why I wanted to leave. It was an idea that had passed through my restless brain during my sleepless night. A practical aid, I hoped, towards solving the mysteries that surrounded me. And in the back of my mind a warning voice added, 'and perhaps save my life!'.

Darkly, with my sketching pencil, I headed a sheet of paper with a name for each member of the household, excepting me; family plus Hannah meant seven names.

Who would want me dead? And Doctor Byford dead?

Grandfather's paper came first. Was he physically capable? The whisky had been a strong enough reason to make him stagger from his chair, and murder would be a very strong stimulus. It was possible for the Doctor to have been pushed from a lower floor window; a level where Grandfather's wheelchair would make him as nimble as anyone, though the evidence of the keys in my room would be a pointer in the wrong direction and I doubted whether the hands that had tried to push me to my death were Grandfather's. Particularly as the balcony in the vines, where I'd been painting, was tiny and unless he'd literally crawled up the steps . . . no, I didn't think it could be Grandfather.

And a motive? Not an obvious one. Grandfather had been at pains to tell me several times, that he was the main one concerned with the search for me and installing me in Dragonseeds. It would be strange if he immediately murdered me and the Doctor.

I didn't want to include Father in my interrogation, but commonsense told me that the seven papers must be filled in without bias.

Motive? Why would Father want to kill me? I doodled an eye, a fraction of its iris visible. It stared up at me slyly. With a rush of passion, I scribbled it out. Motive! I began again. There was a possibility that only Grandfather had wanted me at Dragonseeds, that Father considered Symon his one and only offspring.

I left Father's paper and underlined Hannah's name.

The tiny body hardly fitted the role of murderer, but she knew more of the Tregellas, their weaknesses, loves and passions, than anyone else. I decided, after deep thought, that she was capable of killing the Doctor if she felt she was helping those she loved. Did she include me in her love, because of membership of the family?

Dominic! My heart skipped. That first evening, when he had stepped from the dusk, fear had risen in my throat, then anger at his insolent manner. He had changed towards me after the tile dragon had appeared—my mother's dragon—proving my kinship. But I had to consider honestly whether the first Dominic was the true one. I transfixed the doodled heart, after his name, with an arrow.

Dominic may have resented a new member added to possible heirs, I wrote, in an unsteady hand. Also he had hidden and disposed of the yellow car. And he was, I felt sure, the strongest, both in character and physique, of any of them. I pierced the heart with another arrow, like a witch sticking pins in a voodoo doll.

"Neal," I said and wrote. Charming, amiable, willing to please most of the time. I underlined the four final words, the memory of his fingers crushing my arm still fresh. I had asked Dominic once what Neal did for a living and he'd smiled and answered, 'he works at being a good brother'. Slow to understand his meaning, I had let the conversation lapse and not until later realised that he'd meant Bella financed Neal! Some of Grandfather's mealtime innuendos about Neal needing to marry well, dropped into place after that conversation. But it hardly made him a murderer.

Bella, I wrote, picturing her slow, easy smile. I could not imagine her control slipping, as Neal's had in the Pagoda. She sailed through life, leaving no ripple of discontent when she passed: the routine of the household shared with Hannah with the minimum of effort. Did Bella, under the

surface, wish there had been no Joanna Tregellas née Selkirk
—and me? Was I a threat to her hopes for Symon's future?

Symon? Which Symon should I consider? The new or
the old? Yesterday's Symon, though a child, had in him the
bitterness to murder me. And I'd turned up, an unknown
half-sister, to add to the puppets in Grandfather's Great
Will Game.

Today's Symon was entirely different. Soft-spoken, instead of dumb, with new depth and sincerity shown through
his brush. I had to be honest and admit that last week's
child was quite likely to have pushed me off a balcony.

Spread out in front of me the papers were disappointing.
No facts fitted together to form a whole; to explain a
murder and a near murder. I read them through again. They
were a hotch-potch of impressions, mixed with obvious
facts. I was at fault, not my system.

More than at any other time, at this moment, I wanted
to remember, to have my past, however ordinary, returned
to me. 'If I could remember,' I wrote on one of the papers—
Father's—'I know I should have the name of the murderer.'

Father! He knew something of my former life; why didn't
he help my memory along, instead of constantly advising,
'let it all come back naturally!' Impatiently, I swept the
papers to the floor and left them; banging the door behind
me.

A murmur of voices drew me to the Library, to Father
and Dominic, their heads together over a table top covered
in sketches. The top paper, I saw, showed a tortoise.

Were their papers successful papers? Or like mine, sterile?

I knew I was being illmannered, but my temper had been
building up, even as I descended the stairs; now recalling
my failure again, my anger simmered over.

"Not like that!" I said leaning over the drawing. "Like
this! With the head up!" A few strokes and the animal
was looking up.

"Ruth!" Father burst out. "How dare you! What right
have you to touch my work? Alter my sketch! It was

perfect!"

The anger had gone out of me. "Well no right, Father! But it wasn't perfect was it? Very nice, of course!" I was backing down and dare not catch Dominic's eye. Knowing the fault was mine, yet knowing also that the tortoise was more attractive with raised head. "Father," I wheedled, "be honest. That animal is much more appealing with its dear little head up, isn't it?"

"A matter of opinion, Ruth." I was surprised to hear Dominic enter the conversation and not on my side. "Your Father knows serpentine, you don't. The angle of the original sketch was more suited to carving . . ."

"And she had no business interfering. I'm not a trained artist, but my ideas and sketches have always been entirely suitable. The sales of my Lotus Flowers are still tremendously high, aren't they, Dominic?" He raced on. "I. . . ."

"I can draw too!" I smashed into Father's recital of how good he was. "And paint." I nearly told him that Symon was the genius in the family, then bit it back.

Dominic was re-drawing the tortoise design in red, when Father said, coldly and very clearly, "I can't think why a waitress should be interested in art!"

"Waitress!" I was completely bewildered at this new turn in the argument. "Waitress? What do you mean?" I turned to Dominic. "What does he mean?"

He finished outlining the tortoise, then answered. "You were serving in a small restaurant before you came here."

If I hadn't felt so desperately cut off and miserable, Father's face would have had me in fits of hysterical laughter. I knew exactly what he was thinking. 'I wish I'd never told her about being a waitress' his twitchy fingers told me, plucking a few strands of hair. And because he'd started me scratching in my brain for what was lost, I was spitefully glad that he was torn by doubts, knowing he would have done anything to retrieve the backbiting scene enacted since I had altered the tortoise.

But now my tongue was ready to run free, recklessly,

without heeding possible consequences.

"Someone," I said loudly and clearly, exactly as Father had spoken minutes before, "wants to murder me!"

Dominic's eyebrows chased up to his hairline, Father's face was incredulous. I wanted to cry. I don't know what else I would have said if I hadn't been stopped by the appearance of the entire damned family, just as Father echoed, "Murder!" in a voice that sucked in air, making him choke.

"Murder!" The single word from the wheelchair was unashamedly avid, like an undertaker at a battle.

"We were looking for you," Bella tried to iron out the tension, "to discuss Grandfather's Birthday Party."

"Never mind my party!" The testy command upset any further effort to cover the word murder. "Tell me what your Father's twittering about!"

I was tempted to say, 'One of you, here in this room, can tell the story better than I', but I contented myself with a factual report of what I thought of as 'my Balcony scene'—so very different to the one in Romeo and Juliet. Juliet? The one other person regularly amongst us. I was side-tracked for a moment, but it didn't take more than a few seconds thought to rule out the nondescript Juliet.

No, my would-be murderer was here listening to my explanation of how the vine had saved me and, no doubt, cursing it.

I stumbled to a finish, ending at the point where Father had appeared in the Conservatory and asked me what on earth I was doing.

"Your accident," Bella suggested carefully, "could have . . . unbalanced you a little." She hastened to add, "Only temporarily, of course," and gave me a warm, understanding smile.

A sea of relieved nods agreed with her. They had closed ranks. Swiftly, efficiently, clanishly; even Grandfather's desire for blood and thunder was sacrificed to suppressing crime within the family.

'But it's happening to one of the family!' I wanted to scream; but knew it would be no use.

"Reaction! It could happen to anyone after a blow on the head," Father agreed, running both hands back from his temples.

"I should forget about it, Ruth." Hannah's eyes met mine and I was shocked to recognise pity there.

The situation was cleared to everyone's satisfaction, except mine, They broke the circle to which I'd been a troublesome core and happily returned to discussing a cake in the shape of a tower for Grandfather. I felt like one person on the end of a tug of war rope, against a full team. My feet were slipping and I was being gobbled up by the other side. To my bewilderment, within a short time, I too was giving my views on a tower cake; murder pushed aside to be replaced by marzipan dragons.

The wooden dragons on the Panel nearby continued their saga of emotional friction. Seven of them, nostrils dilated, whispered together.

"They're talking about me," I said to Neal. He almost concealed what he thought, as I continued, "What d'you think of my mental state, Neal? Shaky?"

An unexpected shaft of sunlight found its way between the books to open a doorway of light in his pupils, as he answered: "You're over-sensitive!"

"That's almost what Bella said," I pointed out.

"Oh, Ruth, we're playing with words." He tucked my hand into his arm. "Come on, let's promenade a little."

Like melted butter his charm smoothed and soothed the corners of my ill-humour. I laughed at him. "You're incorrigible, Neal!"

"Good! Let's go and lay the ghost in the Pagoda." Then seeing my puzzlement. "You know? The wicked Neal that slipped out in the dark!"

I threw a look at my cousin as we left the Library. It was supposed to make plain that I considered he'd been a poor ally to me since I had entered the room. His return glance reminded me of Black Adam's portrait, darkly piratical. Certainly not a glance to inspire confidence.

"I wonder how we've annoyed Dominic?" Neal remarked as I walked, toe to heel, down the mosaic dragon.

"I can't imagine!" I replied, stepping down hard, so that my feet made a satisfying slap on the emerald stones; successfully leading Neal's attention from Dominic.

As we passed my favourite Magnolia tree, Neal reached for a waxy bloom. The stem broke with a soft 'cluck' and the branch, with its shiny leaves, sprang back, showering me with rain drops and wetting the backs of Neal's hands as he tucked the white blossom in my hair.

"There, now all you need is a grass skirt," he said dropping a soft kiss on my cheek.

By the time we had reached the Pagoda, the Neal who had alarmed me so in the darkness of the previous night had been completely exorcised. Once again I had a friend; a confidante . . . I hoped.

"It was true, what I said, Neal, about someone trying to kill me. You believe me, don't you?" Just one person to convince here, not seven. When he didn't answer, I said sharply, "Neal!"

Sap from the Magnolia's stem had joined with the rain water from its petals and was running coldly down the back of my ear.

Neal said, "I'll believe your attempted murder story if you'll believe my brother and sister story. Is it a pact?"

I wasn't hearing right, surely. "That's stupid! God, that's stupid!"

"Is it? We know both stories are hardly credible. I want you to believe mine, you want me to believe yours!"

Was he right? Both stories were like something from the Sunday papers, but mine, I knew, was true. Or did I?

Amnesia and tile dragons; people whose lives seemed pre-destined by a Panel; murder; and the important question of who was truly related to whom in a family tied together by forces far stronger than the individuals that made it up.

My head ached. The higher my hopes rose, the lower they fell at new disappointments. Perhaps Bella was right and I was unbalanced, incapable of recognising the truth. Perhaps Neal's story was true.

"I'll believe you," I told Neal wearily, and accepted Dominic as my half-brother.

Returning to the house, I tossed the sticky, drooping Magnolia under the tree. There was just time to wash my hands before going into lunch.

I passed the salad bowl to Bella, watching my own hands. They hadn't carried out the minor task in a particularly deft manner. But it was quite possible I'd been a poor waitress.

Bella arranged the tomatoes, cucumber and lettuce in a neat design around the edge of Symon's plate before passing the bowl to Dominic. The exquisite porcelain salad servers transferred a pyramid of green and red vegetables to his plate. His hands manipulating the knife and fork, were not over-broad, but the fingers were long, with each nail filed to the tip of the finger. Allowing for my nails being longer, there were still quite distinct differences in shape.

What had Marcus's hands been like? And my mother's?

I made my way to the Gallery as soon as I could. I ignored the blue eyes that stared at me from the portrait and instead looked at the hands clasped together in an exaggerated pose, beneath her chin. Her nails? They were rather ugly, I felt, inclined to a squareness that didn't match the pretty-pretty impression given by the rest of the painting.

Marcus's were not shown in his portrait.

Standing, looking at mother's pale features, I was trying to will her into my memory, when I heard a sound at the end of the Gallery.

"Oh good, Symon, it's you!" I said. "Is there a photograph album in the house?"

"There are hundreds of ph . . . photos in the cupboard on the l . . . landing."

"Which landing? Mine? He nodded and I thought how useful a nod was to him to save a word.

He led the way and lifted down from the cupboard a large brightly painted box.

"Would you carry it to my bedroom, please. I'll run ahead and open the door."

I up-ended the box on the floor between us and out slithered hundreds of smiling faces.

"That's Hannah," Symon said unnecessarily, as I held up the picture of a pretty girl, holding the hand of a small boy I recognised as Father. Another boy had turned partly away from the camera to wave at a dainty girl passing by. Marcus, it appeared had always been attracted to women.

I sat on my heels and, one by one, went through the records of the Tregellas at work and play; from babyhood to adult life. Occasionally, I referred to the reverse side of a photo for the date, or Symon would say a name. The tick of the clock was loud in the room, the sound of the sea muffled by the closed windows. Seagulls called plaintively, their shadows crossing the green carpet and darkening the photos as they wheeled past the balcony.

Symon left me, wanting to finish his painting. I continued sorting, laying pictures in lines to compare faces and hands.

Side by side, my Uncle Marcus and Father shared a family likeness, such as brothers rather than twins have. I held a photo of each of them beside me, at shoulder height, and gazed in the mirror. The three faces reflected back to me were laughing; three similar shaped faces framed by thick hair. Here, said my mirror, are two men and a woman who are, probably, related. No more, no less!

Deep in tangled doubts, I almost missed the tap at my door. The photos! Should I hide them? But no, I was family looking at family. So, I opened the door, a mere crack, and Dominic stood there.

"Yes?" I tried not to make it sound too rude.

"Cousin Ruth! Aren't you going to invite me in?" He was wearing his sardonic manner, I noted, with sinking heart, but I stood back to let him in.

A slight draught stirred the shiny squares on the carpet,

rippling them towards the bed. I closed the door quickly and the movement ceased, but still left hundreds of Tregellas faces scattered about our feet, staring at us.

"Ah, you've been going through the family album, I see." He retrieved a handful of the squares and started a neat pile in his hand.

"Hardly an album," I answered, starting to collect the pictures too, but with my mind on that morning when Dominic had made no effort to help me, either with Father or the others.

"Neal believes that someone tried to murder me." The statement as I made it was rather like throwing a glove at the feet of an opponent.

Dominic picked up the glove. "Does he now! Well, so do I!"

"You didn't stick up for me!"

"What was I supposed to say? That you'd previously told me of someone trying to dash you to your death? It wouldn't have been evidence. You have none!"

"Only my word!"

He shrugged. "You heard what Bella said, 'it's all in the mind'."

"It suits the Tregellas family to believe what they want to believe," I yelled furiously, tears burning at the back of my eyes.

His grin was touched with venom. "That applies to you too, Cousin Ruth," he said.

The tears were damned. Through the redness of temper I tried to count ten, but it was useless, the words came;

"A little less of the cousin," I ground out. "I think sister is the word you want!"

I had played my trump in this verbal battle, but I was afraid as Dominic started towards me.

TEN

"Dominic!" Panic echoed in my own ears as I stumbled backwards. "The photographs . . . you're treading on them." Arms outstretched I braced myself against his chest. "Don't . . . " I said, as the bed touched the back of my legs.

Both my hands were imprisoned in one of his as he thrust his body hard at me. I found I was lying on the bed looking up at a stranger. His face came down, nearer to mine, with slow deliberation.

"Dominic, don't!" he mocked. "Don't what?"

The hand trapping my hands was rock hard, the knuckles digging into my breast bone, with his increasing weight. In momentary fear I tried to wriggle free. "You're hurting me!" I managed to gasp.

He lifted himself enough to transfer the hand from between our bodies, only to pin my hands on the bed, above my head. Now I felt his heartbeat pounding against me, and then his mouth, rough, demanding, covering mine, and I knew this was what I had wanted from the beginning.

I lay warm beneath him, responding to his lips. "Ruth!" he whispered against my neck, releasing my hands, so that I was able to link them behind his head, feel the rough texture of his hair.

Reason is outside the vision of this emotion, I told myself, and surrendered the next few moments to unreason.

"Dominic!" I pushed him away from me reluctantly. "At least let's discuss our," I searched for a word, couldn't find it, and said lamely, "relationship."

He rolled away from me, onto his back, leaving the taste of his skin with me. "Which relationship do you mean?

The 'I love you' one or the brother, sister one?"

"Both," I answered honestly. "But it had better be the brother, sister one first."

"Well?" he said, unhelpfully.

"Well?" I said, equally unco-operative.

He sighed, sat up. "I take it you're referring to the supposition that my father and your father are one and the same?"

"Yes!"

"Where did you get the story from in the first place? Oh, I know it's common knowledge in the family; the possibility, I mean. But I did wonder who was kind enough to inform you."

"It was Neal," I admitted.

"I thought it might be. A touch of jealousy, was it?" His profile was all-knowing as he continued without waiting for an answer. "My father, and I repeat, my father, liked everyone. He was friendly, happy-go-lucky; treating the highest and the lowest in exactly the same manner. You can check that by asking anyone; particularly the villagers, they remember him."

"The perfect man!"

"Don't be sarcastic, cousin Ruth. Obviously, he had his faults. He was fond of women. All women. A weakness shared by many men, you'll agree."

I nodded, "And . . ." I prompted.

"And there was never more to it than that."

"How do you know for sure?"

"He was basically a very honest man. He'd admire your mother because she was pretty, he may have been sorry for her, but he would never have stolen his brother's wife."

I did my best to feel convinced. I wanted to be convinced. "Your father was kind and attractive," I said. "My mother was bored, disliked by her new family, and your father was there."

"Does that prove she was unfaithful with him? No, of course not! The whole yarn was pinned on her after she

138

ran away."

"But that meant maligning Uncle Marcus as well. They wouldn't do that!"

But we both knew they would. Within the family it was permitted to tear and rend with words and accusations. To outsiders they would present a united family picture; impenetrable.

I squirmed nearer to Dominic, on my elbows, and dropped across his chest. "Wouldn't it be strange," I said, "if when my memory returns I know the answer. Know who mother ran off with. Perhaps I lived with him until recently. A stepfather? I expect Father would know!"

"And I expect he wouldn't tell you," jeered Dominic, taking the sting from his words by stroking my ear with the back of his hand.

"Father could tell me a great deal if he wanted to," I said resentfully.

"So?"

"Each time I work the conversation round to me in my pre-amnesia days, he says, let it all return naturally. I could scream, Dominic, honestly!"

"Scream away now, my love!" His arms tightened round me, pleasurably, in a vice-like hug. "Let's not think about it any more. We could be doing other things! Nicer things!" He tempted.

"No wait! I've just thought of another point. Why would mother make off in her moment of triumph?"

"Triumph?"

"When she was going to give birth to a new Tregellas. Unless I'm not a Tregellas! Unless my father is the man she ran off with!"

The disembodied other me was returning. Again I was standing back to examine and poke among the debris of my mind.

"Unless! If! Leave it alone!"

But I couldn't. This new angle, the possibility that I wasn't a Tregellas, therefore, unrelated to Dominic, was something that exploded dozens of smaller questions that must have answers. It could be the true reason Father, if he was my Father, evaded my questions. But if he wasn't my Father and knew that he wasn't, why advertise and find me and bring me to Dragonseeds?

"Remember me?" The words were warm on my ear.

It would be so easy to remember only him and discard the mysteries. But Dominic was part of them and underlying the joy I was experiencing with him, was an uneasy sense of danger—a premonition!

"Dominic! What if I'm an impostor? A confidence trickster!"

"With those eyes? You're the nicest one I've met, you and your tile dragon."

His kisses were tickly and most unfair. It was impossible to think myself into the role of a criminal when my arms betrayed me and slipped round his neck.

Later, I promised, I'd go back to my papers, with their headings and disjointed facts and, perhaps, with a little extra information, everything would fall into place . . . later. . . .

It was nearly midnight when I did get out the papers. Should I bother with them so late? Grandfather had been so wearing at dinner.

"Memory coming back yet?" he'd shrilled down the table before I'd settled in my chair.

"Leave her, Father, please!" Father's words were out so swiftly that my own were left unsaid.

"Don't be stupid, Fabian. The girl's healthy enough to answer a civil question."

Were you healthy with a blank where a memory should be? It was a moot point and not one I wanted to argue with Grandfather. So, I answered, "Nothing's back yet, Grandfather. I'll tell you the minute it returns." Like talking of a parcel or a traveller, not a memory, I thought, ladling soup and not tasting it.

"I'll take you into Galston tomorrow, if you like, Ruth."

Dominic said. "If you'd like to see a Doctor there, Byford's stand-in will see you."

"What you need is a shock," Bella laughed. "It's supposed to be the cure for your complaint. At least it is in the books."

"I had one in the Garden Conservatory, thank you," the bitter words were out beyond recall.

Neal, next to me, set down his spoon and cleared his throat. "Oh, you mean the attempt on your life?" he said, and turning to meet his eyes I realised he was honouring our crazy pact. The 'I'll believe your story, if you'll believe mine' one. The pact that was automatically cancelled by me when Dominic walked over the photographs and kissed me. But Neal wasn't to know.

"Did you decide on a tower shaped cake?" Hannah asked Father. But she didn't expect a reply.

"Oh, your miraculous escape from death, you mean!" said Dominic entering the odd conversation like an actor on cue.

And so I set down my spoon, sighed loudly enough for them to notice and related again the details of my fall into the vine.

I started matter of factly and finished with goose pimples raising the hairs on my arms.

"You . . ." began Bella.

"Don't say I imagined it," I warned. "A thump in the back isn't the sort of thing that can be mistaken. No," I was waving my hands like windmills, "someone wants me dead!"

"The cake . . ." Hannah tried hopefully again.

"Damn the cake!" I said violently. I had their full attention at last. "Why?" I asked staring into each face in turn. "Why do you want me dead?" I'd not expected an answer. "Is there some deep, dark, mystery attached to me, that I know nothing of?" I said directly at Grandfather, knowing my sarcasm would be wasted on him.

The focal point changed from my end of the table to

Grandfather's at the head of the table; like onlookers at a tennis match the heads swung back and forth with the conversation.

"No mystery that I know of. You're here." The high pitch to his voice was broken by a quaver of impatience. I think he would have gone further, but Bella said:

"The mystery bit was your Father finding you. He'd advertised before and . . ."

"And got nothing but cranks and impostors," Neal finished.

"Impostors!" echoed Grandfather venomously. "Fancy thinking they could fool the Tregellas."

"And what proof did I supply?" Intense curiosity had diverted me from thoughts of my murder.

Father looked unhappy as he answered me. "Your reply included a photograph. I was convinced as soon as I saw it that you were my daughter."

"And . . ."

"And when I arranged a meeting with you in London, talked with you, and discussed . . . various things, our relationship was confirmed."

'Well, why can't you talk to me, tell me,' I wanted to rave, but stupid pride held me tight and instead of shouting, 'What was so dreadful in the way I was living when you met me,' I said, "And so I was restored to the bosom of my family! Why?"

"Well . . . well, it's only right that you should be here," Father faltered.

"Why?" I repeated.

"Because of my Will! Because of Dragonseeds!" Grandfather's tiny features were alive. "I can't make up my mind, you see! It's only proper that every member of the family should be here when the time comes for my Will to be read." It was obvious that he was referring to an event he expected to be far distant; but the joy of manipulating the strings—his kith and kin—was all important.

The rosiness of Bella's dress cast its warmth on the creamy

skin of her deep chest. Did I imagine the faint pink glow on her face at Grandfather's words? And Symon, surely he felt some emotion, under his introvert's impassivity!

What was Dominic thinking? Dominic who kindled a nerve-tingling excitement in me! Was it just a physical thing I felt? And did love for me lie behind the mask he was presenting now?

The light from the bronze mirrors behind him made a golden halo that edged his features, outlining his mouth in deep clefts of mockery. It was a satanic face, needing only a pair of horns to complete it. He moved his shoulders impatiently and the devilish incandescence was gone.

Grandfather had resumed his soup, well pleased with his part in the proceeding conversation. His eyes were slits, cutting out the light, as he mentally savoured the words just spoken, 'I can't make up my mind, you see!' How glibly the phrase had slipped off his tongue. How many times must it have been thrown in front of this gathering! Now I understood what Bella had meant, 'Grandfather plays a little game with us!'

I looked to Neal. He smiled, but the corners of his mouth seemed not quite steady.

How calmly we drank our coffee together, light conversation filling our ears; malice and murder in our thoughts; the calculating stares of the dragons on us.

"You didn't get far with your murder investigation," said Dominic softly.

"I didn't get an awful lot of help, did I?"

"Why don't you forget the entire thing. Concentrate on living from day to day! Be happy! You're a Tregellas now! Start putting down your main roots!"

"Join the clan is what you're saying in a rather roundabout way. Put flights of fancy from me, see only what it is best to see, and hear, and . . . join the clan!"

"Yes, Ruth! Do it for me . . . please!"

He was stroking a baby dragon with a forefinger and I tensed as though I was being caressed. I knew the message behind his advice. The Tregellas are right whatever they do; murder included. Forget what is gone before and I will protect you, said his eyes.

I made one last effort before surrendering to the offer. "You promised to take me into Galston to see a Doctor if I wanted to. Just a last check to be sure there is nothing to be done about my amnesia."

He smiled agreement. "Be ready after breakfast and I'll run you in. Meet you at the garage at ten. Right!"

Another quick smile and he moved away from me, returning his cup to the tray he disappeared through the alcove.

The promise concealed in the few words I'd shared with Dominic was in my mind now as I sat on the bed shuffling my named papers; my Murder Name Game; there was little I could add to them.

Symon still remained silent in company, though willing and happy to chatter when we were alone. Soon he would be returning to school after the holiday break.

I pencilled in a few more notes. Only a line or two to each paper, mainly confirming their characters.

Under Father's name I wrote, 'How did I get such an indecisive man for a Father?' Then felt mean and crossed it out because I was a bundle of indecision since living at Dragonseeds. Perhaps I'd always had the failing in my 'other' life, without loss of memory to be my excuse.

Opposites must attract where Bella and Father were concerned, I decided, and was overwhelmingly glad that there was a ruthless—or did determined sound better—streak in Dominic, that would ensure any uncertainties in his life being swept aside.

Poor Father made himself miserable with his inability to overcome his own shortcomings, letting off suppressed frustration in sharp fits of temper. Symon's inward facing nature had been inherited from our Father; I hoped passionately that Bella's serenity would emerge eventually in his strange make-up. Symon would never sparkle at any gathering, but it would be nice to think that one day he might contribute a very small joke.

It had been brave of Neal to come to my aid at Dinner. 'Saint Neal!' I wrote and laughed aloud, for Neal, I knew, was a lazy, nearly always charming man, who was working his way round to proposing marriage to me. He would love and cherish me, and any part of Dragonseeds that might come to him, through me, equally.

"Dominic! Neal!" I said as I opened my bedroom window onto the balcony, and their names were lost in the salty mist.

Gulls complained at the disturbance, shuffling patches of whiteness against the cliffs far below. The rocks stretched like humped, black serpents, into the turbulent sea. Dragonseeds even had its own dragons, I thought, and I was still smiling when the wind snatched the window and slammed it against my head.

The scream was my own, I realised, mingling with the screeches of the startled gulls. But the pictures, like water and oil stirred together, were in my head, yet all round me, part of me; twisting and shimmering, until finally a far away voice said:

"Be more positive in your outlines, Ruth! Like this!" And dear old Mr. Minors took my brush and did wonderful things to the painting in front of me; accentuating the lettering on the Inn sign—The Pig and Bottle—in the foreground of the scene, and outlining the signpost that pointed to the road winding over the sun dappled hill.

A dreamy restful landscape. But Mr. Minors and my beautiful painting were fading and instead Father was on the phone to me:

"We'll talk when you get here," he said, and I was sorry he sounded so worried. All the same I answered firmly, "I've changed my mind!" and when he tried to interrupt me, "I've changed my mind!" . . . until the rattling window and the seagulls reminded me that I was semi-conscious on the cold of the balcony floor.

This new bump was quite sizable under my searching fingers. I staggered as I stood up and leaned against the door handle, to shut myself in and for support. I slapped cold water on my face and held a saturated sponge to the bump. With my eyes tightly closed a last picture of the Pig and Bottle was screened on my memory, then wiped clean, as I felt for the towel and dabbed carefully over my latest wound.

"Well, it was your own fault, this time, your balcony scene," I told my sorry looking reflection.

So, in bed, I gave serious consideration to whether the balcony incident above the Garden Conservatory had been of my own doing. At best, I could say I was accident prone, at worst, that I had a strong death wish.

Bella had tactfully suggested that the aftermath of my accident was amnesia plus an over-active imagination. At this moment I was ready to accept that explanation.

It was much simpler, I discovered, snuggling further down the bedclothes, to give up the idea of someone harbouring murderous intentions towards me. Relief submerged the shock and pain of my sore head and I was poised on the edge of sleep, until I recollected the serpentine key-ring, Doctor Byford's death and the yellow car.

I was still wishing I'd never met or heard of the Doctor at breakfast next day. And, having draped my hair over my bump, I wasn't pleased when it parted and Grandfather said, "That's a nasty bump, Ruth. Another murder attempt!" and cackled and choked in his cereal.

Straight after breakfast, I excused myself and went to my room to change. This was my first proper outing, a date, with Dominic, and I wanted to show him I could be an attractive companion. Not the bronze suit I'd worn for Neal, something more feminine; a fluffy lighthearted lilac dress with a scarf belt of blue-green.

It was well before ten when I stepped out of the studded doors to be bathed in warm sunshine. I spared a glance down the grass slopes where the yellow car had begun its fatal journey, then turned my back and made my way round the weathered granite wall of the tower towards the garages.

They were dug out of the rock base of the tower, with long sliding doors to seal them. Lichens spidered in tapestries of colour over the stonework and thrift clung to the crevices. Insects sunning themselves, buzzed annoyance, as I pushed back the end door, so that the white outside light slanted across the dusty floor. Particles danced in the dazzling brightness, rising and falling, as high as the domed ceiling above me. I was surprised at the size of the garages, or garage, for it was one huge chamber, and there seemed a great many vehicles in it.

I switched on the electric light. In the cavern of the inner garage it was yellow and adequate, but it faded and became useless when it reached the sunlight.

Nearest to me, grey and newish, was the car I had travelled in to Galston with Neal. Further over was Father's car, staid and black. A heavy tyred Land Rover type of vehicle was filled with packing cases, presumably in connection with despatching the green serpentine trinkets to various destinations. I sidled between the dusty mudguards and bonnets to a curious van-cum-car; a modified wheelchair conveyance for Grandfather. The next one, I knew, was Dominic's; dark blue, sleek and low, it had a controlled strength, an affinity with my cousin. Several items that I recognised as his were in the open dashboard and his driving gloves were on the seat.

"You are a beauty!" I told the blue monster and walked carefully round it, sliding my hand over the warm body, admiring the fittings. It was when I stooped, peering at the front bumper, that I saw the few strands of black trapped by a nut in the metal. Illuminated by the brilliance at the tail end of a slant of sunlight, they moved gently in a breath of air.

A niggle, a question mark, was triggered off somewhere in the no-man's land of my head as I leaned closer to examine the wisps and hesitantly touched them. It was human hair, I knew—mine!

So the bumper of the car, not the pavement had been the cause of the stitches in my head, I reasoned, with detached calm.

When Dominic came, I was settled in the front passenger seat, waiting.

"Cousin Ruth!" he said softly, against my hair.

It was unnatural to respond so ardently to the kisses of a man who'd almost killed you—most probably on purpose. Living at Dragonseeds affected one's sense of proportion; the Legend of the Panel reached out and swamped you with its haywire values. There could be no other explanation for me relaxing now, and fully enjoying the love making of Dominic Tregellas, whilst seriously considering that he might still want me dead.

I did not let my new knowledge, the black hairs, intrude into my enjoyment of the drive. I had faced up to the possibility of my cousin being my half brother and overcome it. This problem would be solved too, I thought, with optimism. In fact, it was doubtful if what I'd seen was my hair. A quick sight of one or two silky strands caught on a nut. Hardly evidence for the conclusions I had jumped to. Dominic would have stopped if he'd hit a pedestrian. The problem was solved.

The whole idea of Dominic running me down, faded, like the bad daydream it was as we swept past the ivy coloured stone cottages, with glimpses of azure sea and tall slender stacks guarding deserted mines.

"What if this new Doctor won't see me without an appointment?" I asked Dominic.

"Ah, the mastermind has already phoned and arranged it."

I laughed. "Thank you, kind sir! What did you say was wrong with me?"

"I told him you were a bit . . ."

"Unbalanced!" I filled in.

"Not quite yourself yet, after your accident," he said

148

calmly. "His name is Brown and he sounded youngish and pleasant."

He was, listening sympathetically to my description of the wild ups and downs of my temperament; my moods, my imagining. I was cheating perhaps, for he wasn't to know that Doctor Byford's death and a fall from a balcony were involved in my symptoms.

"Have your family remarked on your . . . er . . . inconsistent nature?" he probed.

'It's all in the mind!' That's what my family thought and said. They'd not said I was mental, just mentally unbalanced from the after effects of a blow on the head.

Suddenly, I wished I hadn't come and I wished it even more earnestly through the X-Rays and examinations and 'hmmm!' that followed.

I was still seeing small blobs of dark and light, when Doctor Brown gave his summing up.

"Nothing to worry about unduly, Miss Tregellas! These things take time! . . . the brain is a very delicate piece of equipment . . . amnesia . . . shock . . . your new environment . . . excitable . . . rest . . . a fortnight's time . . . tablets . . ." his soothing manner, even tones, flowed on, until he ushered me to the door.

Nurse Tulk was probably in the building somewhere. Should I seek her out and exchange a few words with her? But no! I was selfish, anticipating the time to be spent with Dominic on the return journey. I would talk to her, another day.

As the heavy doors closed behind me I spotted Dominic, his back to me, leaning against the car. I scuffed my feet in the grit on the drive and he turned, pivoting slowly on his heels.

My smile froze as I saw his face. It was completely taken over by hate and fury.

And it was directed at me.

ELEVEN

My feet faltered, but I forced them on, and as I drew nearer I saw Dominic was regaining control. His eyes were still overbright, his mouth cruel, but the tightness was disappearing. When I reached the car, only the savage way he thrust a paper into his pocket betrayed the degree of restraint he was exercising.

"Cousin Ruth!" he said, and I hated the way he mouthed the words.

What had happened during the period I'd been with Doctor Brown? I was frantic to know, yet retained enough sense to realise it would be unsafe to ask.

It should have been a taste of heaven, the journey home, but instead it was night-marish. I felt Dominic's brooding antagonism, like a third presence in the car.

"Thank you!" was all I could manage as he dropped me at the great doors of Dragonseeds.

I didn't watch him drive round the tower to the garage, but I heard the harsh, unnecessary spin of the tyres as he over accelerated.

"What did the Doc say?" Neal called from the Library as I stepped into the Hall.

"Nothing! Well, not very much," I amended. "He said give it time, and I've some tablets to take."

Why was it that libraries always smelled the same! Old, dusty and musty! Bella and I would really have to work on some of those top shelves, I told myself wearily.

"Did the Doctor upset you, Ruth? You're looking pasty!"

I dropped into the chair next to Neal, desperately forcing myself to recall any detail, however small, that had taken place during the morning and that could have been mis-construed, if thought of later. What had happened to change Dominic so frighteningly?

The softest footfall sounded and Neal said: "Hello, Dominic! There's a cold lunch for the two of you in the kitchen."

I didn't look up. I heard Dominic say, "I'll have mine later," then came a creak from the nearest chair to the Panel and the skid of his heels as he let his feet splay out in front of him.

Some of the day's mail was still on a tray. It brought back a picture of Dominic pushing a paper or envelope into his pocket, outside the Nursing Home. Not this morning's post, it hadn't been delivered when we started to Galston. Yet the feeling was growing that the paper was the clue to the incredible transformation in Dominic's attitude.

I would have to know what was written there!

The mustiness in the room was stifling. Stronger where the sun drenched the older books. I felt choked. Why hadn't I noticed before that the Panel was made up entirely of evil beasts! Almond eyed, lustful creatures with unclean thoughts.

"Grandfather's having a Pagoda cake," Neal laughed. "Hannah and Bella were talking of dragging you into its preparation."

"Good!" I said, dully, and as Neal's eyebrows rose in a questionmark, "I'm just a bit depressed. Apparently loss of memory can go on for years. I shall have to start and make up a past for myself to replace the dud one."

"Funny thing, loss of memory!" There was a bite in Dominic's tone. "It's hard to disprove, isn't it?" If it suited them anyone could say they'd lost their memory!"

There was no doubting his meaning. Uncertainly, Neal, said: Oh, you mean it would be a boon to schoolboys. Better not let Symon hear the idea or it will be a case of, sorry I've forgotten all last term's work."

My head was throbbing. Could be there was a storm

gathering in the nearby hills, moving closer. It felt like it. In the hallway, the telephone started a shrill, earpiercing demand to be answered.

Dominic made no move. His face was impassive, his eyes gleaming with an expression I'd so often seen in Grandfather's eyes—malevolence!

"It's for you, Ruth!" Bella called.

I was reluctant to pick up the phone. "Hello!" I said, in little above a whisper.

"Oh, Miss Tregellas! We must've passed in the corridor this morning. I'm so sorry. . . ."

"Nurse Tulk! It's you! I was sorry not to see you, but I had to hurry back home," I lied.

"I went out with the ambulance, unexpectedly," her voice rushed on, "But I gave the papers to Mr. Tregellas. Hope that was all right!"

Papers?

"Yes," I answered automatically, "Yes, thank you!"

"It was lucky I was helping Doctor Brown to go through Doctor Byford's desk and papers. They were in the back of a drawer. He'd put them in a clean envelope. Left it unsealed and, of course, I realised at once that the one sheet was the last part of your letter from your Father. That lovely thick paper. No mistaking it. Pity it's so dirty!"

"Yes, a pity," I agreed. "It was clever of you to spot it was half my letter though."

"Goodness knows when you'd have had it back otherwise, if ever!" Nurse Tulk continued. "I expect it's been in that drawer ever since you were brought in. Ambulance man handed it to him, I expect." Her mind veered off: "Any improvement in the amnesia?"

"About the same, thank you." I made an effort. "I'd love to see you sometime when I'm in Galston."

Her pleasure zoomed along the wires, making my ears ring. I was ashamed of being glad when she said she must go.

"Good news, Cousin Ruth?" He was leaning casually

against the inside of the Library alcove, and I guessed he must have heard me mention Nurse Tulk by name.

That olive green sweater suits him, I thought, and decided that Bella was right and I must be mad to consider Dominic being attractive when I was both angry and afraid of him.

"Give me the papers!" I said, and my voice came out as a loud hiss.

Very slowly he made a pretence of searching his pockets, before taking a folded paper from his back pocket and holding it out to me.

I took it quickly—snatched it—afraid he might withdraw his hand at the last moment. Yes, it was the second page of Father's letter to me.

"Nurse Tulk referred to the papers," I said, but I spoke hesitantly, unsure now.

His eyebrows rose a fraction as he shrugged. Without a word of thanks I walked away from him. It was an effort to mount the stairs, knowing he was standing there, still watching.

Safe in my bedroom I took the original Dragonseeds headed letter from my bedside table, then lay on the bed to read the two pages together. The first sheet said:

Dear Daughter,

I can hardly believe you are coming to me at Dragonseeds. I've told my Father, your Grandfather Justin, everything that was said when last I met you and he is excitedly looking forward to your arrival.

To think that if Father had not insisted on another advertisement in *The Times*, after all these years, I would never have found you . . .

The second sheet continued:

. . . and had the future to look forward to.

I am glad you realise it would be better for all of us if we didn't discuss your mother. What is past is finished and she is dead.

I know you will be happy here. We are a close family. The letter ended simply: Father.

There was a P.S. with mud and oil nearly obliterating it. I switched on the table lamp and held the paper over the light. The words became clear.

Don't forget to telephone me at Galston 27821, from the long bus stop—the last one before Galston—to confirm all is well.

The two sheets of paper together said very little. A rather stilted letter from a father to his newly discovered daughter; a welcome, nothing more. I examined the second sheet again, word for word, there was nothing in it to account for the change in Dominic. There had to be another paper.

"What shall I do?" I asked my enigmatic green man, and decided for myself. One of Doctor Brown's tablets would relieve the tension building up in me.

Lying on my bed, searching for the answer to my problems, I found after five or ten minutes that I was appreciably more relaxed. I recited a list of my troubles out loud and my stomach didn't curl any more. I thanked God and Doctor Brown for the miracle of the small white tablet. The only side effect was a hint of sleepiness; sketching would help me overcome it. Not scenery; I'd have to go out of my bedroom. No, something from memory. From deep in my memory. The scene that the bang from the balcony window had produced. The Inn with the swinging sign; The Pig and Bottle and the dreamy sun-filled lane that ran from the crossroads with its lopsided signpost.

It was startling how the picturesque scene grew under my fingers; names on the signpost; a slat missing from the gate in the cottage adjacent to the Inn. Even Mr. Minors seemed to be repeating, 'Be more positive in your outlines, Ruth!' A voice without a body.

I hadn't felt well enough after the sad business of my visit to Galston with Dominic, to eat the salad that had been left for me. But I certainly had not intended to sketch my way past afternoon tea. If Father had not come fussing in to see what was wrong, I would have started painting my scene.

"D'you like it?" I asked, standing it on the floor near the window's stronger light. When he didn't reply immediately, I turned to him, surprising a look of disbelief on his face. "Am I better than you expected?" I quizzed hopefully, the unfortunate incident with the tortoise sketch still with me.

"It's good! A very high standard!" he said, rather jerkily, ruffling his hair. "In fact I like it very much indeed." He smiled, a quick nervous smile in response to my delighted beam. "I don't suppose you would consider presenting it to me! I would value it! Have it framed!"

Was it partly Doctor Brown's tablet suppressing unhappiness, building up goodwill? Or was it genuine Father, Daughter warmth that was rushing over me? I tore the sketch from the pad and gave it to Father; happiness welling up in great sentimental spasms. I wanted him to stay; needed to talk to him.

"Have you a few minutes to spare, Father?" I said. "You know there are so many questions I want answered."

He was undecided, unhappy at the prospect of a discussion with me. So before he could give me a definite no, I pushed my stool towards him and flopped on the floor beside it.

"I've tried to put you off, Ruth, as you know. I know there are questions that only I can answer but, believe me, they're better left until . . ."

"But the gaps are driving me mad! I may never recover. I want my past and my present tied up in one togetherment. You can supply practically both, can't you?"

"Leave it, please! Only a day or two more!" He had jumped up and was making for the door, rolling the sketch.

A few days! I could wait until after Grandfather's party, then broach the subject again. Or ask Grandfather? He must know my history too! Or did he?

"Thank you!" I said, and closed the door gently behind Father.

Re-inforced by a quick nap and a second tablet, I was

able to face up to after dinner discussion.

Hannah, who had been looking tired, was brighter to-night, I was happy to see. Neal said as much.

"That's because of her wine tasting." Grandfather joked from the far end of the room and I marvelled at his ability to carry on a conversation and eavesdrop on another yards away.

"I'll fetch Hannah's brew!" Dominic unfolded from a nearby chair and walked with studied care round my feet. When he returned with a tray heavy with bottles and upturned wine glasses, I'd tucked my feet well beneath the chair.

Bella spread the glasses and bottles over two lacquered tables, while Hannah, pinkly happy, poured a little wine into various of the glasses.

Neal dragged a stool against my chair and set a glass on it.

"What shall we drink to?" he asked, raising his glass so that splinters of light, backed by the wine's rich glow, winked at me.

"We can't drink to Grandfather's Birthday until the actual day," came from Bella.

"How about toasting Ruth?" Dominic had returned to his chair. I couldn't see his expression, but an arm was bran-dished aloft, the glass tilting so that its contents lapped near the glass's lip. "To dear Ruth's memory! Sorry! That makes it sound as though she's dead and gone, doesn't it? Let me say instead, to the speedy return of Ruth's memory!" And the liquid slopped in a red rivulet down his wrist.

"To the speedy return of Ruth's memory!" chorused those about me, startled, but not particularly caring who or what they toasted.

My glass, held high in acknowledgement, trembled slightly, as I carried it to my lips and gulped half the contents at one go.

"Steady on, Ruth!" Neal laughed. "Hannah's homemade stuff packs a kick."

"Too late!" My eyes were watering. "What is it?" I

gasped.

"Plum, or it may be elderflower, but I'm more inclined to think it's a mixture thing!"

I took a wary sip of the potent wine, a sniff at its deceptive fruitiness. "Are the others like this, Neal?"

"Some even more so. Hannah's been at it for years. We always have wine tasting before your Grandfather's party. It's supposed to be to choose the one wine for the occasion, but we invariably finish up with the lot."

The hum of the wheelchair announced Grandfather's arrival. "What d'you think of it, Ruth? Good?" His wheels shoved aside the stool acting as my table as he edged closer. "It's going to be a Birthday picnic. A lunch! Tomorrow! What about that?"

"Lovely!" I said, draining the last drop of crimson and wondering if it was wise to drink home made wine on top of Doctor Brown's tablets. I would ring the Doctor in the morning, before the picnic, and find out.

I watched the tiny figure in the sheepskin shoes, bustle between the chairs, filling glasses. "See if you like the dandelion wine," she said, filling my glass and Grandfather's.

Some comment was expected, so I said, "Mmmm!" in an appreciative way and she moved on, satisfied.

It hadn't the sweetness of the first wine. Perhaps it was more mature. Or was it sweeter when it was new? I gave up bothering my head over such a minor matter and instead sipped and talked to Grandfather, who, I was distressed to see looked decidedly blurred.

"You're wuzzy round the edges!" I told him. "And you've got pleats in your face!"

It was obvious they all possessed Grandfather's knack of carrying on a conversation and listening to another. Now they let their own gossip die and moved in to listen to ours.

He laughed and the pleats opened and then repleated, and I had the feeling he was not laughing with me. But there was real amusement in his voice when he said, "That's what happens when you're seventy-five and ill! Could be

I'll never see another Birthday!"

'God!' I thought, I've started another silence. Dragonseeds was all mealtimes and silences.

Someone said: "You'll live for ever!"

Whatever had amused Grandfather was gone. "Live forever! I wish I could! In Dragonseeds! Because it's mine!"
His squeaky voice climbed higher. "If I live forever, then
Dragonseeds will stay mine! You won't get it! Any of
you! It's mine, until the last breath leaves my body!"

Somewhere, Symon sniffed.

The wizened face darkened and then cleared as he peered
at me. "You're a nice girl, Ruth!" he said surprisingly. Then
his chair became alive as he switched a knob and raced
across to Hannah. "I'll have a bottle of each," he commanded, "for the party!"

The hum of conversation resumed and merged with the
sound of Grandfather's chair as it sped down the room,
ricochetting off the edge of the Panel. The dragons looked
contented today, I saw. Perhaps they were affected by the
wine.

I was deadly tired when I wished the family goodnight
and still sleepy when I awoke the next day at seven to
soft mist at my window.

We hurried through breakfast, all of us, and despatched
a sneezing Juliet home until the pollen count subsided and,
therefore, her hay fever.

"Well, that's one pair of hands less," Hannah said and
returned to the shaping of the Pagoda birthday cake.

We'd decided on the party menu earlier and we now
double checked. The Aspic Jelly had been prepared and was
poured over quartered, hard-boiled eggs, prawns and cold
vegetables. Hannah, long before breakfast, had filled small
dishes with jelly and Bella had concocted a huge trifle, in a
cut glass bowl, doused in sherry and topped with creamy
whirls and cherries.

Fat pastry envelopes filled with apples were cooling
when Dominic and Neal put their heads round the door at

eleven, arguing about the arrangements for taking cutlery
and pickles down to the picnic site. I reminded them that
the icecream was to go down very last thing, before slipping
away to take one of Doctor Brown's tablets to ensure my
continued tranquillity. No one was going to have cause to
call me unbalanced.

The sun was warm on my hands as I washed melons and
avocado pears and tied them in polythene bags. The two
men returned pushing a garden trolley and we loaded
gurgling bottles of wine and a hamper.

And no word of love or hate passed between Dominic
and me, even when Neal smiled his irresistible smile and
blew me a kiss.

As the Party time drew near, I saw Dominic pushing
Grandfather's chair across the courtyard.

"Quick! Time to change!" I called to Bella and Hannah,
running for my bedroom. "No time for a proper wash," I
told my little green man as I shed my clothes and took a
saffron coloured dress from its hanger.

I gave a last look at Grandfather's present—my painting
of the view from the Garden Conservatory—before wrapping it.

I'd hurried, but the others were ahead of me, piling the
grassland with fruit, unpacking glasses.

"Happy Birthday, Grandfather!" I said, handing over my
gift and kissing his dry, papery cheek.

He undid the paper, said, "Good! I like it!" then, "What's
that bit of yellow in the distance, there?"

"It's gorse!" I told Grandfather firmly, trying to recollect
when I'd added the Doctor's car to the background.

"Isn't any there!" he said, exultant. "You'll have to
paint it out!"

I promised to and risked a glance at Dominic, close by.
There was nothing in his face to show that he had disposed
of the yellow blob, over the cliff.

The party finished unpacking, laughing, slithering on the
uneven ground. I looked to Bella where she lolled like a red

flower on the bank.

"It's worth all the trouble," I called.

I discovered a comfortable grassy bump to rest against. I relaxed completely, chasing a cherry round my dish and hazarding a guess as to the type of wine Neal was pouring for me. I sipped, wriggled my tongue in the first mouthful, then guessed, "Plum?"

"Elderflower!" Neal laughed and departed with the bottle.

It was like a summer's day with the sun beating hotly through the leaves, provoking thirst. I took a large sip, then another and another. Disregarding the tickly grass I lay back, fumbling for a place to rest my empty glass. The wind stirred the foliage above me, parting the branches, so that the sun broke through into my eyes, blinding me. With my lids tightly closed, for some reason I remembered I'd not phoned Doctor Brown about any side effects from combining his tablets with Hannah's bottled juices.

With my head to the earth, a footstep sounded near me. I looked up into Symon's face. Silently, he held out a chicken joint, then went.

My glass, balanced beside me, had been refilled by someone. I sat up and tasted the new offering. It was sharp, this one, almost bitter, and it lacked sparkle.

"Drink up, Ruth!" Hannah appeared. "Home made wines are full of goodness! They ensure long life!"

Under her watchful eyes, I swallowed. As she moved away I poured the rest surreptitiously over a daisy plant and wiped the sediment from the bottom of the glass with a heart shaped leaf.

I was thankful when Father brought a bottle clearly marked Plum Wine and filled my glass.

"Lovely!" I said, drinking, then, "Oh, the icecream! I must fetch it! I'll use the big tray to save Hannah coming with me."

The slope from the picnic seemed steeper than usual. I'd eaten too much. Or was it lying in the sun that caused my feet to drag and the outline of Dragonseeds to lose its shape and break into colourless fragments!

The kitchen wheeled like a merry-go-round and the insects from the picnic were still with me, deafening me. "I'm ill!" I said aloud and remembered again the call I should have made to the Doctor.

Grandfather had a small den, with a telephone, leading off the Conservatory; that was the best place to go.

The insects were thunderous and I was having to think hard about moving each foot. I'd never be able to return to the picnic with the icecream. Had I taken it from the fridge? I couldn't remember!

Dropping in a chair in the den I willed myself to pick up the phone. Grandfather could do with more light in this room. On such a day it should be radiant, polished with whiteness, not grey. I pushed the papers that filled the space between my hands and the phone, and at that precise moment Dominic spoke.

"What are you doing here, Ruth?" he said softly.

It was a swivel chair, needing only the tiniest movement to bring it about so that I faced him in the doorway. But because of the room's greyness he seemed a faceless ghost.

"I'm going to phone," I explained, my tongue dragging.

"But you came for the icecream. I heard you say so!"

"No . . ." Was it the icecream? "No . . . I . . ." There were black threads over my eyes. That must be it! The threads—my hair—on the bumper of Dominic's car. No, it wasn't that either. It was the paper! Yes, the second paper! Dominic had it!

I said, as clearly as I could, "The other paper, you . . ." then remembered it was the call to Doctor Brown that was so important. "Doctor Brown . . . I need him. . . ." I told Dominic urgently, as he moved closer.

Why were my phone calls so unsatisfactory! There'd been the call from Nurse Tulk and those bits of telephone conversation with Father that leaked back to me. "I've changed my mind!" I'd told him several times.

Dominic was standing over me now, closing out the last of the light.

Very loudly, I said, "I've changed my mind!" as the room melted into black icecream.

TWELVE

The tubular bedrail with its chart, carried me back to that earlier time; it was the same room. This time I didn't have to say 'hospital!'.

"Feeling better, are we?" I had Nurse Tulk in attendance again.

"Could I swill my mouth out?" The words were woolly, like the inside of my mouth.

When Nurse Tulk balanced me against her arm, I flopped, and my mouthful of water, intended for the bowl, spattered us both.

"I'm accident prone in more ways than one!" I muttered. Then with fuller awareness, I added, "I ache all over!"

"Stomach pump," she answered briefly. "It saved your life though."

I'd been in Grandfather's den, hadn't I? With Dominic hovering like a black bat! Had I taken the ice-cream from the fridge? Such a pity if it had melted. Grandfather liked chocolate flavour, with spoonfulls of cream stirred in. Was he cross at my interference in his Birthday Lunch? 'How dare you die in the middle of my ice cream course!' I fancied him squeaking.

Somewhere in that den scene and its aftermath, I could recall the nurse friend of Dominic's; the one who had snipped out my stitches. She'd been wiping my face and I was being sick. And there had been a mad drive and the smiley Doctor Brown, minus his smile and . . . God, yes! . . . the stomach pump.

"I intended to ring the Doctor about taking my tablets with wine," I said.

163

"Mmmm!" It was a queer look I was getting from her. "You overdid it, didn't you? But never mind now. Rest a while. You can have visitors later."

So I rested until Neal came with roses and a grave, hospital face.

"Cheer up, Neal, I'm not dead yet!" I told him and he winced.

The smooth charm I associated with Neal had deserted him. When he left after five minutes banal conversation I was dispirited and knew nothing of the family except that Father was not well and unable to visit me.

Nurse Tulk was bed patting and surprisingly untalkative, when Dominic appeared.

She was by the door in a second, arms spread, tutting: "Too late for visitors now."

He smiled gently down at her, and a few words drifted across to me: ". . . minutes . . . Father unable to come . . . family . . . kind of you. . . ." And he was in and my Nurse blushingly confused, closed the door as she left.

He was pale, I saw, and I felt the blood drain from my own cheeks as he approached silently. The bed creaked as he leaned, arms stiffly braced on the bedrail. A fly zzzed angrily on the window, loud in the stillness, and my own quickened breathing seemed equally loud.

"I'm sorry, Ruth," he said. "I didn't want anything like this to happen!"

A twinge of fear fluttered in me; whatever he meant I was surely safe here, where a scream would bring Nurse Tulk.

"How . . . what do you mean?"

"Your tablets; you could easily be dead now!"

"Yes, I . . . go on!"

"The food stopped them acting so quickly and you were dreadfully sick."

"And don't underestimate the stomach pump," I said mechanically and wished I knew the direction this conversation was pointing.

Quite suddenly, the fury that I knew lived in Dominic,

164

erupted. He had my wrists gripped so tightly, so painfully, that I threw myself backwards, straining away from him.

"You fool, Ruth! Did you think I would give you away? You must have known I wouldn't!"

His words were accompanied by a vigorous shaking that snapped my head back and my teeth together. Weak tears started down my face and seeing them Dominic released me.

"Oh, Ruth, Ruth! I wouldn't hurt you!" Only seconds before he had. Now I was folded like a limp, white doll, over his heart.

Bewildered, I accepted this new, kindly, Dominic. "I don't understand!" I confessed against his chest.

"You're not well enough to discuss . . . upsetting things. We'll sort everything out when you return to Dragonseeds."

I was so very willing to leave everything if it meant replacing it with Dominic's kisses. They started tenderly, on my temples, then joined my lips, moving on with grow-passion to my neck . . . my shoulders . . .

"Miss Tregellas!" said a scandalised Nurse Tulk from the doorway. "You'd best be going Mr. Tregellas. We don't want the patient excited!"

"I'll fetch you soon, Ruth. Don't worry!" And he was gone.

But I did worry. My short period of knowing myself had turned full circle. I was back in the bed whence I had started my new life. I would insist, yes insist, when I was home, that Father tell me all he knew of my past life. He did know, I was sure. It was he who had inserted the advertisement in *The Times*, on Grandfather's behalf, as he was always at great pains to point out. But he had met me, talked to me, knew my former life.

I laughed, recalling Bella's advice—a shock—for curing amnesia. If a shock could have cured me I would surely by now be in full possession of every single detail I so desperately wanted.

The telephone on my bedside table gave a short ring. "Miss Tregellas? an impersonal voice enquired. "Mr. Fabian

165

Tregellas for you."

"Father? Are you better?"

It was a bad line, his voice was slurred, but I heard him say, "Much better, thank you!" And ask how I was feeling.

"Oh wuzzy! But Neal and Dominic have been to visit me. Dominic is bringing me home soon." I waited. "Are you still there?"

"Yes!"

"How is Grandfather?"

"The same as usual!" He sounded nearer. "He's talking about his Will." There was a low rumble of thunder overhead, blotting out Father's voice. ". . . Dragonseeds," I heard him say as the roll of noise flowed away.

"What did you say?"

This time I saw the lightning, more brilliant than the daylight, imprinting white window panes for a split second on the walls; "One . . . two . . . three . . ." I counted, then the crash and roar was magnified a thousandfold. The surface of the water in my glass shivered.

"Father," I yelled down the phone, "I can't talk to you, there's a storm. Can you hear it? I'll be with you again soon, goodbye!"

As I finished Nurse Tulk came in.

"Not frightened are you?" she asked. "I'll stay with you a bit, if you like." She settled in the visitors' chair, large and kindly. "D'you want to tell me your troubles?" she said, in a pocket of quiet.

Troubles! To which troubles was she referring? Or was she being companionable? A faint whisper of unease, starting up, settled when I remembered her face on discovering Dominic and me in the warmest of embraces.

"Oh, Dominic, isn't trouble," I laughed. "The contrary, in fact!"

Whiteness bathed the room, as she started to answer me. "Then why. . . ." her mouth opened and closed, but a tremendous clap of sound above us, wiped out her words.

"What did you say?" I screamed, my throat sore and

aching.

"Why did you try to kill yourself?"

I heard, yet didn't immediately comprehend her meaning. I started to laugh, then stopped abruptly as the words finally sank in.

"I didn't! Of course, I didn't!"

She was embarrassed, poor woman, but determined to continue. "Then why were you so full of the tablets that Doctor Brown prescribed for you?"

"I don't know! I didn't take them on purpose! My God! Is that what everyone thinks!"

She nodded and would have spoken, but the phone rang. "It's for you," I said.

The storm and Nurse Tulk leaving the room became a backcloth to my chaotic thoughts. What had I thought was wrong with me? Food poisoning, I supposed, I had thought. It was ludicrous, even to me, to realise I hadn't thought, had not had time to think, of the reason for my being here. I had swilled out my mouth; talked to Neal; made love with Dominic and spoken to Father. Then the storm had struck and Nurse Tulk had sat on my bed and calmly asked me why I had tried to commit suicide.

"I want to go home!" I whimpered into the pillow, as the storm crashed away from Galston, leaving me clammy and afraid. For I knew, without doubt, that murder was stalking me again.

I lay awake through the night, listening to the rain, hearing the first imperious notes of a black bird at dawn. And at ten, Dominic came. I thanked Nurse Tulk for her care and left against Doctor Brown's advice.

"Why Father's car?" I asked, as we left the Nursing Home gates.

"More comfortable for you," he explained. "Though the darned thing's not dependable."

We were on the cliff road when he said quietly, "Want to tell me all about it, Ruth?"

I sought for a thread to start unravelling. "What do you

want to know?" I asked carefully.

"Well, start at the beginning. From the phoney amnesia bit."

Phoney amnesia! That was what he thought?

I turned from him, looking seawards to the granite sabre teeth grimacing through the curtain of rain. My fingers explored the ridge where the stitches had been. "My amnesia is real, Dominic. As far as I'm concerned my life dates back from the Nursing Home—the first time." The engine note changed. "What are we stopping for?"

Only the sea sounds and the water streaming down the windows, hammering on the roof, remained, now the car was idle. Warmth from Dominic's arm, as he slid it along the back of my seat, permeated my hair. His eyes raked almost to my soul, it seemed as I stared steadily at him. It was a relief when he slumped back in his seat.

"So you don't know anything of the second letter?"

"No, no! How can I know?" I said, adding, "So there was another paper for me from Nurse Tulk. What did it say?"

"It was a letter. . . ."

"Can I see it?" I asked swiftly.

"Do you trust me?" He countered quickly; a question instead of an answer.

My lids sank together and immediately memory used the darkness to project pictures; Dominic of the cold face, at our first meeting; Dominic driving the Doctor's car to destruction. The hairs—mine—moving in the warm air currents, pinpointed by the sunlight, attached to the bumper of Dominic's car. And other pictures too; the flagstones of the Garden Conservatory floor whirling to meet me, as I fell, and the sediment I had wiped from my glass.

At least one had time to think during sleepless nights. Those, endless, bitter hours had told me that the sediment in the wine was the second murder attempt on me, at Dragonseeds. And too, I'd had time to sort out the disjointed phrases that I'd blurted out in Grandfather's den. I'd spoken of the second paper, then mentioned Doctor Brown. 'I need him!' I'd told Dominic, and finally, 'I've changed my mind!'" It was no wonder that suicide had been the most handy and probable answer.

"Do you trust me, please, Ruth?" Dominic's grip on my arm was urgent.

"Yes I do!" I said, and could almost hear Bella whispering 'unbalanced'.

No other words passed between us, as he started the car again, forging into the blinding rain. Near Dragonseeds, I asked uneasily, "Is it often like this?" as water rose in two great wings from the bonnet of the car.

"It hasn't been this bad for a long time. They'll be flooding, I expect."

There was. Great lakes of it on the flat roads, waterfalls as we climbed higher, until we were home.

An hour later I was sitting in a red leather chair, drinking honeyed milk.

It's all happening again, I thought.

They were very kind considering the general impression was that I'd tried to kill myself and in the middle of Grandfather's Birthday Celebrations too.

I could explain to them that it was another try at killing me, but it would be a waste of time.

Grandfather said gruffly, "We'll soon have you well enough to help with the meals again." The nearest, I supposed, that he was likely to get to hoping I was better.

Father was vague; distant, and looked pasty. Perhaps I should tell him the truth, that I'd not tried to kill myself. But not now.

I was served an invalid's meal on a bronze tray. Symon was a silent audience of one, perched like a pixie on the arm of a chair. I didn't try to engage him in conversation now that I knew him well. Instead I smiled and received a small, quick grin in return. I let my range of vision widen to take in the names of the books near his shoulders. 'Poisoners Through The Ages', inscribed blackly on a red

169

binding drove home to me the events of the last few hours. I pushed the milk pudding away from me in sudden revulsion.

I badly needed a food taster, I thought bitterly. From now on, I would guide my wobbling legs to the communal table, so that the same food would be shared by all of us.

And so I found myself on my usual bench in the Conservatory. I declined the sugared flowerheads that were Bella's speciality, because they were being eaten by no one else, nibbling instead a twist of pastry. Normal conversation was practically impossible because of the pummelling of the rain on the glass roof, like the sound of frying through an amplifier.

Beyond the Conservatory was a great wet nothingness. Just outside my vision I could imagine the willows bending to their full extent, the blossom trees tossing wildly. The narrow, gentle stream that meandered through into the bridge pool would be muddy, wide and enraged. Could the rock plants nestling in its shallow banks, hold out against the destructive rain, or would the rocks above break loose and start a chain reaction of tumbling and flooding, down to the meadowlands?

Light poured in in a great flash, showing the stark faces round me. Within seconds an ominous growl of thunder followed. As one clap ran into another Symon dropped the biscuit he had been crumbling nervously and Bella, crossing to him at more than her usual pace, crushed it under foot. The crumbs scattered with her final step, making a powdery arrowhead. I would have landed there, from the balcony, if it hadn't been for the vine.

I shuddered and the sensation was more extreme because of the tremors that accompanied the storm.

"I'm going to my room!" I shouted, mainly for Dominic's benefit, and left the staring faces.

Bed! I took off my top clothes and crawled between the sheets in my underwear. I had hoped for sleep, but every nerve seemed to have crept to my finger tips and my physical need was overridden by this nervous instability.

I lay, trying to keep my mind empty, until the premature darkness of the storm was lost in the natural darkness of the day's end, then I heard the telephone ring in the hall below.

There was the rise and fall of a man's voice. Other voices called to each other, excited, fading away as their owners left the hall.

"Ruth, Ruth! It's Bella! Open the door!"

I snatched my dressing gown from the door and let Bella in. "What's happened? Is it to do with the storm?"

"Yes! Flooding! At Juliet's! Her mother's crippled. We're going down to help, Hannah and I. And the men too, of course!"

"You can't get down the fields! Will you go by road?"

"Yes! Dominic has already gone and taken Symon. Neal will drive Grandfather."

"Grandfather's going?" I said, unbelieving.

"He's insisting, and actually his van may be useful to put Juliet's mother in. We shall all be needed, Ruth. You'll be safe here." And she left me at almost a run.

I sat on the bed, seeing nothing. Poor Juliet and her Mother. And poor me! Who someone wanted to kill! 'You'll be safe here!' Bella had said and then they'd all gone and left me alone in the belly of the Dragon.

"I'm going down to talk to the Panel," I told the green man, dragging a spare blanket from the cupboard. Better to doze in the Library until the rescuers returned.

I half walked, half slithered, leaning on the bannisters, swathed in my blanket. I rested on the bottom step, poking the mosaic dragon with my toe, before trailing into the Library. As I passed the screen the lights dipped, hesitated, then recovered. Without further thought I switched them off and felt my way towards my favourite chair. Re-angling it so that I had my back half to the wall, yet still partly facing the dragons, I perceived they had their evil faces on. Or was it imagination and the constant flicker of the lightning burnishing their wooden snouts, creating a three-dimensional tableau, symbolising Dragonseeds and the Tregellas.

Crazy me! Seeing in ornately fashioned carving the life cycle of the family. Because each of my relatives was made up of so many characteristics, it didn't mean they were going to destroy themselves eventually, didn't mean that I would destroy myself. But in the next crash of sound I pictured again Nurse Tulk's face, her lips mouthing 'why did you try to kill yourself?'.

A sound nearby that didn't belong to the storm made me look up quickly, and I gasped, despite myself.

"Ruth!" said Neal, and I saw his uneven outline against the screen.

"Neal," I answered fearfully. "What . . . what is it? What do you want?"

"My fishing waders. And I slipped in to see if you were keeping calm. Sorry, if I scared you!"

"No, of course you didn't. I could see it was you." I laughed loudly to prove it. "You haven't brought Grandfather back with you?"

"Not a chance! He's enjoying every minute of it down there. Sitting with the back of the van open, in the dry, shouting orders that no one listens to. I've had to borrow Dominic's car. If I scratch it he'll murder me."

With a wave he was gone.

A good half hour later, when the vast orchestration of noise was reaching new heights, the second shadow fell on the screen.

"Is that you Neal?" My voice was shrill enough to rise above the elements, for the figure, I knew, wasn't Neal.

"It's me!"

It was a husky voice that I couldn't identify until Father stepped forward.

Relief spread through me and I relaxed into my blanket. "Oh, Father!" I said, "Neal's been for his waders. What have you forgotten?"

He didn't answer, but dropped heavily into a chair opposite me, making a small pool of light as he switched on

He smiled at me. A wan smile. "That's what I'm doing," he said. "Or rather, trying to do!"

"Good! Now what did you come back for?"

"An axe!" He lifted it from the floor, where it had lain in the shadows.

I could imagine they would have need of it in the debris carried down by the flood water. Down at Mrs. Helston's cottage. But I would have thought there would be enough tools among the helpers already there.

"Don't go again," I said, concerned by his strangeness.

"I'm not going," said the man who was Uncle to me now. "I returned to . . . to do a job. Something that has to be done!"

"Yes!" I prompted.

"I'm sorry, Ruth!" And there was true sorrow in his face. "I'm sorry but I've come to kill you!"

THIRTEEN

I had never noticed before how loud the tick of a clock could be. The insistant tattoo of sound from the Library clock above outside noise, pecking like a bird at my brain.

"What did you say?" I asked stupidly.

"You've got to die, Ruth. It was arranged from the start. I'm sorry!" he said again, begging me to understand.

"But why? Why do you want me dead? I haven't done anything to you . . . I. . . ."

"No, no! It's nothing personal . . . please understand . . . it's Father's fault . . . his games. . . ."

"You're ill!" I soothed desperately. "Why don't you rest? The others will be back shortly and. . . ."

"No, they won't return yet. . . ." His hand cast a shadow on the blade; the other hand, fingers restless, worried his hair into strands. But the usual urgency of his movements was blunted, there was a dreamy quality, a haphazardness, about him.

The use went out of me. The clock's tick returned to normal. "Tell me about it, Father!" I said dully, and wondered if he would question my use of the word, 'Father'.

Fascinated by the tap of his fingernails on the axe's blade, as he sorted in his mind for the direction his story should take, I shrank deeper, seeking comfort, between the fatness of the chair's leather arms.

"It was Joanna's fault," he began. It was never his fault. "Joanna's fault," he repeated. "Father never forgot that the baby Joanna bragged of must be walking about somewhere, Tregellas blood in its veins, belonging here. Another possible heir to wave in my face—boy or girl—it didn't matter."

176

Bewilderment, combined with cold terror held me spell-bound, listening.

"He went on and on about it, until in the end I found an Investigator; a London man." His lip curled with distaste. "Not a nice person, but he didn't make his money on nice cases. He found you for me. . . ." The sentence hung, unfinished, though his lips moved silently.

A crazy disassociated thought entered my head. Would it be easier to kill a niece than a daughter, if you had a desperate reason to kill!

"We found each other! What then?" I tried to be calm.

"We talked. Don't you remember? Arranged about the advertisement in *The Times*!" The fingers that massaged the middle of his forehead shook. "No, of course, your memory!"

"You wrote to me," I reminded.

"Yes, the two letters. I arranged it so beautifully and then, at the last minute, you rang me and said you'd changed your mind."

Those few words on the telephone to me, completely out of context, had returned to me. Useless on their own. "What had I changed my mind about?"

"Coming here! Staying here! The phone call from the last but one stop was just to confirm that all was well. And it wasn't. You said you would continue into Galston and then go back. You'd changed your mind!"

"I'm sorry," I said gently, to my would be murderer. "Go on!"

"It's always been the same. Marcus arranged things and they were right, but not me . . . even the mushrooms. . . ." He collected his thoughts with an effort, his face brightening. "And then I was lucky for once."

I was sweating in the blanket, but I remained still as he continued.

"I was parked in the little car park, at the end of the bus station, near the telephone kiosk, when you stepped off the coach. I started driving slowly towards you, to meet you,

you understand. And you walked from the back of the coach. I hardly realised I'd run you down until I was on the far side of town."

"You ran me down?" The room was full of noises and flashes that had nothing to do with the storm.

"It was a heaven-sent opportunity. I took it!"

I fingered the scar under my hair. "But I had a hard head and didn't die!"

"No, you didn't die, but your loss of memory was nearly as good . . . as useful. I brought you to Father because I knew in the end you must die."

"And you pushed me from the balcony above the Garden Conservatory and you fixed my wine at the picnic." It was a statement. I didn't expect an answer. "And Doctor Byford?"

"He knew! At least he guessed the truth about you! It was because part of a letter I'd written to you . . . he had it . . . and he'd got the paper with all the details on. I had to make up my mind quickly . . ."

"But . . ." I said, not understanding.

"I asked him up to your bedroom, said you needed attention and . . . and he went over your balcony and down into the sea."

The remembered touch of the serpentine keyring, against my foot, dropped as the Doctor had fallen to his death, caused the hair on the back of my neck to bristle. I wanted to ask if he had run the Doctor's car into the trees near the bottom fields, but it would lead to questions in return; would involve Dominic. My 'Father' must have been a very puzzled man when the yellow car had been found at the bottom of Gull Cove.

I still thought of him as Father. Not Uncle, or Murderer, and, probably because of the shock of the situation, I was once again looking over my own shoulder, surveying the two of us with complete, or almost complete, detachment.

He was speaking again: "That Investigator, a nasty person, charged me a great deal of money and, of course, there

178

was the money for you."

"Money for me?" I recalled the thick wad of notes in my purse wallet. "But why? and where did you get it from?"

"Haven't you guessed?" he said, childishly pleased. "By selling things. Father has always kept me short of money, so, I sold things."

"The Pedlar!" I exclaimed. "You stole it! And you would know private collectors willing to buy, wouldn't you! Poor Symon! With his odd habits, moving things, I expect it has covered for anything you have taken."

The thunder and lightning had ceased; only the heavy rain continued.

"I'll put the lights on," I said, easing myself forward, pushing the blanket from me.

"No!" He turned sharply to me and the blade shone blue.

I cringed back into the shroud-like blanket. I'd made a mistake. I searched for a subject to start him talking again. Anything to gain time.

"Tell me about the river," I said. "The flooding. Is it dangerous?"

"The flood water!" he whispered and the blade shook. "It swallowed them up, Marcus and Jane! When the ferry rope snapped Marcus grabbed and held fast to one of the broken ends. It was enough to keep the boat afloat." He laughed. A dry, mirthless sound. "You might say their lives hung by a thread! Jane was screaming for me to pull them in, but Marcus was already dragging them in, hand over hand, an inch at a time, towards me on the bank."

"And you tried to help! And failed! How dreadful!"

"Failed? No! The rope was very hard and wet, I remember. I couldn't undo it from the post."

"But you didn't need to!"

"You're quite right! I cut through it with my penknife. Marcus had been laughing up at me, through the rain and the river spray. He wasn't afraid! So sure of himself! Sure of me! I expect he stopped smiling when I loosed the rope, but I didn't notice because it burnt my fingers. The rope, I mean! As I cut through the last strand it shot away from me . . . fast . . . very fast!"

"You killed them!" I said, and doubted now whether the family would return from their wading and rescuing in the village in time to save me. For how much longer could I encourage a murderer to divulge his thoughts, his motives to me?

"It's Father's fault!"

Fear was almost pushed aside as the familiar phrase was brought out.

"He sits in that chair, watching, poking at our feelings. All these years he's said he couldn't make up his mind about Dragonseeds, who should have it. He's talked on and on about Joanna's baby, perhaps a boy, another heir to flaunt. Always Joanna's baby. No promise to me, his son, as his heir."

"And Dominic?" I said hesitantly.

"Dominic is Marcus's son. He has some right to Dragonseeds. A very small part," he said grudgingly.

"And me? Have I no right? Is there no portion of Dragonseeds due to me?" I had not meant to ask, but the words were said.

His hand moved and I was blinded as the flexible arm of the table lamp was swivelled and its glare thrown full in my face. Before I could cover my eyes the lamp's direction was changed again, its beam widening over the short distance to the Panel.

"Your rights?" He was astounded. "You have no rights!" His laughter rose in steps of incredulity.

When he walked across to the Panel, I noticed the axe went with him. He pushed the steps I'd used for reaching the top shelves, in front of him.

"Your rights!" The words and insane laughter continued as he climbed the steps and fumbled, one handed, with the horns of a slit eyed dragon. "Damn!" he said savagely, and then, "damn, damn, damn!"

Restricted in his movements, he hit viciously, with small

chops of the heel of the axe, at the dragon. As I stared, he reversed the blade and at the next stroke chips of the carving sprayed to the carpet; one shiny brown fragment, an eye, lay looking at me.

The unnatural scene, during which I'd sat without trying to escape or protest, was being made more horrible now as the chopping became more maniacal. The blade was landing wildly since its first dragon target had been destroyed.

"What are you doing? Why are you destroying the Panel? Father!"

But no words of mine could stop the brutal hacking, the mutilating of the Dragonseeds saga. It seemed, helplessly watching, that the destruction of the Panel was his object but, as the pieces continued to rebound around me, I felt that he was searching frantically for something. Or rather, at first he had been searching and I had not seen it, now he was striking out in frustration, not intending perhaps to destroy.

A splinter of wood pierced the back of my hand, drawing a bubble of blood. I barely noticed the pain.

There was silence. Father was down the steps and moving them along, nearer the right hand side of the Panel. A great part of the central carving of the Dragons was gone; the wood that remained was flat and pale as though it had bled. The axe recommenced, great clefts appeared in the bellies of sleeping animals, wings flew for the last time as they were dissected by the blade.

Suddenly, there was a difference. A hollowness under the thud of the axe. Father heard it too and slashed the harder.

His scream of triumph shrilled above the sound of falling dragon fragments and then was drowned by a metallic rumbling . . . and the Panel slowly opened.

I heard Father's shout, "There! It was jammed!" before I saw the steps quiver and his hands grab at emptiness to balance himself. The axe arc-ed above his head, he cried out, and they fell together. At the same time the Panel stopped and light from the table lamp reached out a weak ray to touch the contents of the hidden room.

As I comprehended what I saw, a great sickness welled up in me, and I screamed and screamed, until I found myself choking with the effort to express my horror more loudly. As the light ebbed and darkness claimed me, the clammy folds of the blanket settled round me.

The strips of wood were the ceiling of my bedroom. I had almost expected the clinical whiteness of the room where I'd opened my eyes on those two other occasions.

"Hannah!" I said recognising the tiny head. Then moving my own head a little, "Dominic!"

"Ssssh! You've had a shock, Ruth!" said Hannah. "Lie still for a while!"

I was on top of the bed, still in my underclothes and dressing gown, a blanket over me; not the damp shroud from the Library. I shuddered and tried my voice again. "Father?"

"The dragons killed him!" Hannah was crying quietly, the tears finding the lines in her face and filling them. Her body looked smaller than ever as she turned and left the room.

"The dragons! Dominic! What does she mean? Is Father dead?"

"She shouldn't have told you yet!" He sat near me on the bed. "Yes, he is dead! A splinter of wood pierced his eye...." His voice trailed away, leaving me to remember the arcing axe hitting the Panel for the last time. The dragons had killed him! A claw or maybe a needle sharp snout, amputated by the blade, had stabbed him to death.

"Now listen to me carefully, Ruth! There's no time for morbid thoughts. Tell me exactly what happened. Afterwards I'll tell you what we found here, when we returned."

What had happened? I probed tentively at my memory.

I had sat, wrapped in my blanket. Neal had called back for his waders and then gone, and a little later Father had returned too, and stayed . . . with his axe. I told Dominic in short bursts of words, not very clearly, as the events of the evening fell into place.

"He said you had no rights and then attacked the Panel?"

"Yes! I didn't know that the Panel had jammed. I thought he'd gone mad. His manner was so strange from when he came into the Library. He said he had to kill me!" I stopped a moment, remembering. "And then he attacked the Panel, and hacked and chopped . . ." I could not go on to tell of the hail of pieces, of fangs, wings, eyes, as they'd been dismembered from their bodies. "Dominic, it was so vile! The dragons! He slashed them to bits!" My throat was closing again, strangling me.

"Stay calm, Ruth!" Dominic's voice came from a distance. "You're getting too worked up! I would have left all this until morning, but I must have our story prepared!"

I drew in a great gulp of air and tried to concentrate. The massacre of the dragons—the Panel—was still uppermost in my mind and Father's death . . . 'Father's death!' repeated a voice that was inside me, then, 'Father?' questioned the same voice. Something was scouring my brain; memories—not recent—were seeping back, like cuttings from a scrapbook. . . . I was in London, I knew, with Father. . . .

"You saw behind the Panel, didn't you, Ruth?" Dominic's persistence cut off the returning pictures.

Had I seen behind the Panel? I didn't want to know, to talk about it!

"What did you see?" His voice was rough.

I swung my head away from him. Sweat was gathering between my neck and the bed cover and the hair tugged sharply when Dominic's fingers dug into my cheekbones, forcing my face towards him again.

"What did you see?" He repeated.

"Joanna! It was Joanna . . . wasn't it?" The whimpering voice was totally unlike my own.

I brought up my hand, nearest to Dominic and pushed at his hand, alarmed at the vice-like hold. His fingers relaxed slowly, gently slipping into my hair.

"Yes, it was Joanna!"

"I only saw for a second . . . yet I knew! I knew! How long has she been there? And where . . . where is she now?" I said fearfully.

"She's been there since she disappeared. By a trick of fate the conditions between the old wall and the Panel were suitable for preserving the body, mummifying it." He paused and stood up. "Neal and I have disposed of . . . it."

Somewhere, I knew, there must be a coffin-shaped piece of ground with freshly turned soil.

"Doctor Brown is on his way here, Ruth, but, of course, there will be an inquest. And questions!"

"Questions? What shall I say, Dominic? The truth would sound incredible!"

"Exactly! And bring up matters best kept in the family. You must say that you stayed in bed in your room, while we were away. That you were still not well."

"Wouldn't they expect me to have heard Father in the Library? The chopping and banging!"

"The walls are thick. You will say you heard nothing. That you slept, despite the storm, and knew nothing until we all returned."

"Will they believe me?"

"With Doctor Brown's medical testimony, yes, don't worry any more. He was, after all, killed accidentally, and accidental death will be the verdict. Now I must go! There are a number of things to attend to."

I hardly heard the door close. I blotted out the present and allowed full rein to my returning memory. It was being churned up, I was aware, as a result of the violence of the last few hours and the evidence of violence from two decades before.

. . . I had been in London with Father, and another man. A shifty man, with greasy moustache and knowing eyes; the Investigator that Father had said wasn't nice. . . . Slowly, with only tiny patches of not knowing, my past returned to me. Without further drama my life prior to

184

Dragonseeds was united with the present.

How long had I lain, delving, re-examining? Many hours! Through the remainder of the night and into the new day, judging by the light and the smell of bacon. It was difficult to appreciate that the floods, the killing of the dragons, and the discovery of Joanna had all taken place during the previous evening and night.

"I must talk to Dominic!" I said aloud, sliding from bed, fighting a moment of dizziness before shedding my dressing gown. Legs trembling, I dressed and left my room. My feet slowed as I reached the foot of the stairs, but I turned and followed the mosaic dragon.

The Panel of Dragonseeds, that had guarded Joanna's body, was closed, its legend wiped out by the axe; a wall of splintered wood all that remained.

I bent to retrieve a small shape from the ugly pile of chippings that had been roughly swept under a coffee table. It was the small, chubby dragonet—Hope—his claws still sheathed. My fingers were still caressing it, in my pocket, when I found the family in the Dining Room.

"Good morning!" I said huskily, from force of habit, and habit made them answer me, though we were all aware of the empty chair between Bella and I.

Was it bravado that made them heap their plates with food? If so it was highly unsuccessful, for, after cutting the bacon and sausages into irregular pieces and pushing them backwards and forwards, the meals were abandoned, uneaten.

The feeling that we must bring our troubles out into the open, speak of them, hung over the spasmodic outbreaks of meaningless conversation that rose, then died.

"I knew Joanna was dead . . . long ago!" It was Hannah.

A mew of sound came from Grandfather Tregellas, but our attention stayed with Hannah.

"In the secret room? You knew? Who else knew?" Bella's usually rich voice was cracked, her cheeks pallid and lumpy against her unaccustomed dark gown.

"Black Adam told his son of the room's existence, I believe," Hannah looked to Justin Tregellas at the head of the table; a shrunken figure, motionless, low in his wheelchair. "The twins found the means of opening the Panel by accident, when they were climbing up the bookshelves. They couldn't keep the secret to themselves, they were only little boys. They told me! No one else, I'm sure!"

Symon knocked his fork to the floor and I jumped, as did the others.

Hannah heard nothing and continued: "Once in a while, when the house was quiet, I used to open the Panel and look in the hidden room. I don't know why really!" Her tear blotched face twitched. "I must have found Joanna soon after she was put in there. I saw the wound on her head, that had killed her, and the ridge tile dragon was thrown down beside her."

"Did you know who had killed her?" I asked gently.

"I felt it had to be one of the twins. Which one, I didn't know, until you arrived and the tile dragon that Joanna was presumed to have taken with her appeared in the hall niche, with the second one."

I recalled the fresh hand prints in the thick dust on the top of the book shelves, where Fabian Tregellas—'Father'— must have leaned his hand recently, when he opened the Panel for the first time since killing Joanna, to retrieve the tile dragon that was supposed to prove my membership of the Tregellas clan. Had the sight of the mummified thing that had been Joanna driven his shaky mind over the borderline into madness? If so, it was allied to cunning, for he had managed to hide the tile dragon in my suitcase at some time during his visit to me at the Nursing Home.

I thought of the mushrooms that didn't pay and Marcus who did everything so much better and more easily than his twin.

"Perhaps he felt there was some danger he might lose his share of Dragonseeds," I said.

Attention swung from Hannah to me.

"What do you mean?" Justin's voice was tiny, immature.

"He said you played games with him," I explained, and knew by the tightening of his lips that he understood. "So he produced me," I continued, with a bitter laugh, "Joanna's baby."

"But Joanna couldn't have had a baby, she was dead!" Bella said, still not understanding.

"No, Joanna never had her baby, but she died because she was pregnant." I glanced at Dominic. "She told Fabian that the baby was your father's—taunted him with it—and he hit her with the tile dragon."

"But you answered the advertisement in *The Times*," Bella persisted.

"No! Fabian and his Investigator put the advertisement in after they'd found me—right age group, right appearance—and talked me into doing it. They went to a great deal of trouble to convince me it was a very involved family joke that would only last a short time."

"Practically a one night stand!" Dominic entered the conversation. "I presume you were meant to die the moment you were established as the long lost daughter of Joanna. Grandfather's lost heir, a girl, exorcised for ever. What happened to alter the plans, Ruth?"

"I think I'd known all along I was being lied to for some reason. I was uneasy! Then when I was actually on the coach getting closer to Galston, I became more worried. Instead of telephoning to say all was well, from the kiosk at the last stop before Galston, I told him I'd changed my mind."

"And . . ." prompted Dominic.

"He could hardly get his words out, I remember. He said I'd taken the money for 'the impersonation', he called it. I told him I was coming into Galston to return the money and then going back on the same coach."

"And he agreed to that?"

"He said, would I think it over again. I hadn't even got to change my christian name. I would still be Ruth, but

Ruth Tregellas, instead of Ruth Maddison."

"So you're a genuine Ruth!" Dominic smiled gently, and then asked: "Did you discuss it with anyone? Your family?"

"No!" I shrugged. "Secrecy was the main stipulation with the plot, and the only family I have close at hand, is a distant cousin in London. My father married again after mother died. He's a Civil Servant in Singapore. He never approved of my Art Studies and certainly wouldn't have liked me adding to my grant by working in a Restaurant at the weekends. The pay wasn't very good but. . . ."

"But you still intended to return the money?" Bella said.

"Oh yes! I was bringing the money back when fate played into Fabian's hands and I finished up with amnesia." I tried to laugh, but my lips trembled.

I heard the scrape of a chair and through blurred eyes saw Dominic passing Justin and Hannah and Neal, until he stood behind me, hands on my shoulders.

"He ran Ruth down with my car," Dominic said. "His own car was playing up that day and he borrowed mine."

"Then Nurse Tulk handed to Dominic concrete proof of me being an impostor. When I got off the coach I was still holding two letters. One, a very formal 'father to daughter' type of letter, that would be suitable to show at Dragonseeds and. . . ."

"The second page of which you lost," Dominic said, "together with a second letter. It wasn't a letter really, more a formula—a mass of family details—everything that Ruth needed to be a convincing Ruth Tregellas for a few days. It was really a confirmation of what Ruth and Uncle Fabian had already discussed, I presume, and was certainly meant to be destroyed."

Someone asked, "Was the second letter signed?"

"No," Dominic answered. "It was too dangerous a piece of paper for him to put his name to, but I recognised the writing as soon as I saw it. By the time Ruth had been given her check up by Doctor Brown, I had worked out that we had another impostor on our hands."

There was silence round the table. Hannah was crying again, I saw. Bella and Neal were equal in their impassivity. Symon caught my eye and, surprisingly, gave me a warm smile. He and his father could not have been close. In fact, I couldn't remember hearing Fabian Tregellas ever address his son.

Justin was messing with the controls of his chair, so that it bucked noisily. "Doctor Byford . . ." he began.

"We shall never know for certain," I said slowly, "but during the night I've tried to put together all the information, the odd half phrases and ramblings, that Father . . . I mean, Fabian, told me last night. I'm sure, in my own mind, that the Doctor, knowing the family so well, even about Grandfather's Will Game, and that there had been impostors in the past, reached the same conclusion as Dominic. He read the half letter and the other paper and decided Fabian and I were in it together. . . ."

"And he must have come here to face Uncle Fabian and tell him what he thought," Dominic suggested. "Perhaps he was in the area and decided to come on the spur of the moment, otherwise, it seems more likely that he would have brought his proof with him, not left it in his desk drawer."

Listening, I agreed that the Doctor's murder was probably not premeditated, whereas my murder had been planned and gone awry. The murder attempts had been tried hastily when I had said or done something to make my 'Father' feel unsafe.

My tit-bits of returning memory had worried him. 'I've changed my mind!' had been the words to make him push me from the Garden Conservatory balcony. And I'd nearly died when he'd seen my very detailed sketch of the Pig and Bottle. I now knew that this was our last meeting place. Where we had sat and finalised our plans for me being Ruth Tregellas and I'd accepted the money for 'the impersonation'. After I had drawn this scene he'd crushed the tablets in my wine.

Two murder attempts—no three! I'd almost forgotten

being run down in Galston.

Poor Fabian Tregellas! Worrying, scheming; convincing the family that, because of my amnesia, I must be kept in complete ignorance of the make believe past he had provided for Ruth Tregellas. It was so involved, when my own memory had played so many tricks; sometimes throwing up real background, like my Art Teacher, Mr. Minors, whose voice had come back to me with the mental picture of the Pig and Bottle. And the false memory that gave me my first glimpse of a man in a wheelchair, as he'd been described to me.

All so involved! So futile!

Movement drew me back to my surroundings. Hannah had stopped weeping and was gathering the plates together. Incredibly, Bella stood up too, collecting cutlery.

"There's cold chicken for lunch," Hannah said as she left with the tray.

Within minutes the room had emptied, except for one person.

"What are you going to do?" I said to Dominic, pushing back my chair.

"Joanna is dead! No purpose will be served by showing she is dead! And Fabian Tregellas died by accident. Certainly a very strange accident, but nevertheless, accidental death will be the verdict."

He was so sure of himself, the future Master of Dragonseeds.

"And me?" I asked diffidently, stroking the small Hope dragonet that I had rescued from the remains of the Panel.

"You my love?" His smile was sardonic, but his eyes were tender. "You Cousin Ruth, will marry your Cousin Dominic and live happily ever after!"

And his hand joined mine over the sheathed claws of the tiny Hope Dragonet.